Pete Watche___ ___ank a Leaf from Sarah's ___ ___, Holding It over Conn___ ___ead Like Mistletoe.

The light bounced o___ ___
Newby pulled her c___ ___
gave an angry twist. ___

He dove back into the yew bush, and something smacked into the glass over his head.

Pete snapped up. A small hole surrounded by a spider web of cracks had appeared right in front of his eyes. Inside, Newby was gone, Connie was gone, everyone in the room was fleeing the window and crying out. Pete trampled into the yews, pressed against the window, and peered inside.

Newby Dillingham lay on Sarah's braided rug. Connie was bending down over him. Pete's off-balance mind ran through several grisly explanations for the scene but none of them as grisly as they should have been until he saw the neat dark hole in Newby's temple. . . .

Books by Sally Gunning

Hot Water
Under Water
Ice Water

Published by POCKET BOOKS

ICE WATER

A PETER BARTHOLOMEW MYSTERY

SALLY GUNNING

POCKET BOOKS

New York   London   Toronto   Sydney   Tokyo   Singapore

An *Original* Publication of POCKET BOOKS

POCKET BOOKS, a division of Simon & Schuster Inc.
1230 Avenue of the Americas, New York, NY 10020

Copyright © 1993 by Sally Gunning

All rights reserved, including the right to reproduce this book or portions thereof in any form whatsoever. For information address Pocket Books, 1230 Avenue of the Americas, New York, NY 10020

ISBN: 0-671-76005-X

First Pocket Books printing January 1993

10 9 8 7 6 5 4 3 2 1

POCKET and colophon are registered trademarks of Simon & Schuster Inc.

Cover art by Jeffrey Adams

Printed in the U.S.A.

Dedication

*For Tom, again, with love and thanks
for making all this water travel smooth sailing.
May you someday have this same effect in real boats.*

Acknowledgments

Special thanks to Christopher J. Dolan for the forensic research, to William "The Younger" Whitelaw for everything-I-always-wanted-to-know-about-bullets-and-should-have-been-afraid-to-ask, and to Glenn Wilcox for so patiently educating this amateur sleuth in the way weapons work. Chalk up any technical errors to the pupil, please, not the teachers.

More special thanks to Annie Claybrook for all the hours she's donated to the cause, and to William "The-Not-Quite-So-Younger" Whitelaw for being so good natured about the demands of my "hobby." Thanks also to Bruce McFarlane for the miscellaneous firearms facts, and to Steve Shook for the tree on the roof.

Last, but not least, thanks to both my families for all their help and encouragement. I'd like to specifically thank my mother, Nancy Carlson, for reading, proofing, and editing, my brother, David Carlson, for the miscellaneous consultations, my brother-in-law, Mark Gunning, for providing an island tour as well as a Northeaster, my sister-in-law, Mary Ellen Keiser, for her services as secret agent, and my father-in-law, the expert marksman, Thomas J. Gunning.

ICE
WATER

Chapter
1

Peter Bartholomew lay on his back under the Christmas tree wishing he hadn't rolled up the cuffs on his best red Pendleton wool shirt—his exposed forearms were riddled on all sides by pine needles as he rotated the tree in its base.

And rotated it.

"More to the right!"

"Don't turn it, tilt it!"

"To the left. No, no, no, turn to the right, tilt to the left!"

"Too far, too far!"

"It was better before."

Pete stopped turning, tilting, and otherwise adjusting the tree altogether, but not much to his surprise, the crowd at Sarah Abrew's annual tree-trimming party kept right on kibitzing. *Left! Back! Right! You had it a minute ago . . .*

The hell with it. Pete began to surreptitiously tighten the wing nuts, a half turn at a time, around and around the rickety old tree stand, ignoring the voices swirling over him and concentrating on their shoes instead.

Pete could tell by the shoes what kind of people these were, what kind of party this was, what kind of mood each was in. Sarah Abrew wore her favorite festive red ones, heels too high for a woman in her eighties, the doctor, Hardiman Rogers, was just now telling her. The doctor's own L.L. Bean Comfort Walkers were well worn from the endless treks between his office and his patients' houses, and he hadn't wasted time on fresh polish. Pete's business partner, Rita Peck, wore the soft brown leather boots that only came out for best, but Rita's sixteen-year-old daughter, Maxine, wore her dirtiest sneakers, the ones she always dragged out whenever her mother's boots appeared. And standing close beside Rita's boots were Evan Spender's galoshes with the old-fashioned metal clips, the galoshes a tribute to Nashtoba's traditional December rain, the green corduroys above them a tribute to the spirit of the occasion. And the practical low-heeled pumps that flitted from shoe to shoe could only belong to the conservationist Evelyn Waxman—Pete could hear the crackle of her latest petition, for a moratorium on waterfront development, as it floated by above the shoes.

At a distance from the others was a pair of bulky suede boots that Pete had never seen before, and there were Paul Roose's police-issue black ones. The police boots passed the suede without stopping and left the room; Pete's attention was brought back to the suede. What was it about those boots? There was something familiar about them, something about the way their owner stood with the weight on the toes as if poised for flight.

Pete sat up, but since he had neglected to remove himself from under the tree before he did so, he was poked in the eye with a pine needle; and something about the juxtaposition of feelings—intimacy followed

2

by intense pain—brought it suddenly to mind whose boots those were.

Connie's.

His ex-wife's.

Pete lay back down under the tree and hunched his knees in with him.

"Where's Pete?" That was Sarah.

"Over there. Hey, nice tree, Sarah!" Jerry Beggs's hiking boots approached the red heels and he rattled the ice in her glass. "You look about due for another!"

That meant Jerry was due for another, and several people around him, hearing the sound of rattling ice, began to rattle their ice also, but Jerry's trip to the bar was postponed by Evelyn Waxman's petition.

"Jerry, I don't believe you've signed yet. Here, use my pen. I'll hold your drink. Let's not let the bulldozers have the last word, shall we?"

"I haven't signed a petition since my antiwar days," said Jerry.

"Think of this as another war, Jerry. Even more important, I'd say. I'd say that, yes. The sand dunes versus the bulldozers, Jerry. A war, Jerry. Wonderful. Merry Christmas, Jerry. Wonderful." Evelyn Waxman's mind went so fast she tended to repeat herself so that others could catch up. Apparently successful in getting Jerry's signature, Evelyn's pumps hopped on, and Jerry's boots moved off toward the bar.

Pete stayed where he was, in one of his favorite childhood Christmas places, under the tree looking up. Sarah's knobby old tree lights shot starbursts through the branches, the cracked and mellowed wooden ornaments bobbed and swayed with each passing body, the familiar smell of the pine woods dropped over him like a blanket. It was nice under there. There were no ex-wives with puzzling behavior under there, there were no raised eyebrows following the two of them around the room.

"Where the hell is he?" snapped Sarah, and this time it was Connie who moved up to the old woman and answered her more politely than the question seemed to call for.

"I just got here. I haven't seen him. Do you need some help?"

Connie.

Of all the things she had been, she had never been polite. After nine years of marriage she had run away with Glen Newcomb without a backward glance at Pete. True, she had come back last year without Glen, and she had watched in uncharacteristic silence as Pete first hid from her and then confronted her with rage. She had finally, at great cost, Pete knew, attempted an explanation that had forced him to see that things were not so black and white, not so right and wrong. So what was the matter? Was it this new, mortal politeness that was spinning him straight back into his hiding phase again?

"Pete!"

It was Sarah again. Pete scrambled out from under the tree, careful this time to guard his eyes from the pine needles, from Connie, from the rising and falling eyebrows scattered around the room, but it was the ancient and half-blind Sarah Abrew who saw it all and, seeing it, understood.

Sarah's fingers, gnarled with arthritis, clutched him below the biceps with deceptive strength. The red shoes set off purposefully through the crowd of flashing teeth and flushed faces. "The lights. The outside lights. Fix them, for God's sake—they're going on and off like a diner in downtown Providence."

Pete went out alone into the December damp, wading into the wet yews that framed Sarah's living room

4

window. He fished around among the foliage until he found the end of the extension cord, but as he straightened up and looked through the window at the soft light and friendly faces he stopped, the cord forgotten in his hand.

There was Newby Dillingham, talking to Connie.

Newby. Somehow it figured that Connie would get herself involved, conversationally at least, with one of the two most controversial people in town. Newby Dillingham and his older brother, Ozzie, owned a small bait and tackle shop on Close Harbor, but the more congenial Newby was the one who ran the bait shop while the cantankerous Ozzie captained the charter fishing boat. It was an arrangement that suited everyone, especially the brothers, who found themselves embroiled in near fisticuffs every time Ozzie stayed on land too long or Newby was forced to fill in as mate at sea. The brothers had somehow managed to remain bruise-free until Nate Cox, the island's new realtor, had presented them with a $500,000 offer from an off-island development corporation, Connor, Rice and Peterson, less affectionately known to the locals as CRAP. Ozzie had voted to sell out, but Newby had wanted none of it, and there the matter rested, with the rest of the island as much at odds over the issue as the brothers themselves. Pete looked around for Ozzie but couldn't see him, and neither could he remember his shoes. Nate Cox was absent also, which was fortunate for Sarah's party, since Evelyn Waxman's petition was still circulating swiftly around the room. Reluctantly, and yet inevitably, Pete's eyes gravitated back to Newby and Connie as they laughed together in the center of the room.

So this is how it is now, he thought—my life out here, hers in there, neither of us able to break the pane and cross to the other side. But how hard could it be? He could walk back inside. He could wish her a Merry

Christmas. That's it, he'd wish her a Merry Christmas. He'd ask if she was going home to New Jersey this year. He'd . . .

It began to drizzle, and still Pete stayed where he was, the flickering string of lights forgotten as he stared through the mullioned panes of glass at his wife. Newby turned obligingly as people spoke to him, answering each with a friendly word or smile that spoke his pleasure at their company, and Pete thought how odd it was that such a man could have a brother like Ozzie. Newby's gray head continued to nod left and right, but a casual hand on Connie's arm kept her by his side. Oh, he was no fool! Pushing sixty, maybe, more than twenty years Connie's senior, maybe, but he could still charm a bird from a tree. Assuming the bird was looking to be charmed, of course. Pete watched Newby yank a leaf from Sarah's philodendron, holding it over Connie's head like mistletoe. The light bounced off Connie's pale brown hair and slid down the clean planes of her face as Newby pulled her close and kissed her, and Pete's guts gave an angry twist. No, he wouldn't go back inside. She left him, after all. It was up to her to let him know that she wanted him back inside.

He dove back into the yew bush, and something smacked into the glass over his head.

Pete snapped up. A small hole surrounded by a spiderweb of cracks appeared right in front of his eyes. Inside, Newby was gone, Connie was gone, everyone in the room was fleeing the window. Pete trampled into the yews, pressed against the window, and peered inside.

Newby Dillingham lay on Sarah's braided rug. Connie was bending over him. Pete's off-balance mind ran through several grisly explanations for the scene but none of them as grisly as they should have been until he saw the neat dark hole in Newby's temple.

Pete raced back inside and through the buzzing guests. Dr. Hardy Rogers had by now joined Connie on the rug next to Newby, his thundercloud eyebrows pitched together in concentration as he barked out orders first for a blanket, then for the ambulance, then for the deputy, Paul Roose, but Pete left Newby to the others and jumped instead for Sarah. Sarah Abrew, whose eighty-six years had danced youthfully through the long evening, now collapsed into old age before Pete's eyes, her hands trembling, her knees giving way. She teetered sideways. Pete caught her by one arm, and suddenly Connie was there to catch her by the other. Connie pulled her leather jacket off the back of the nearest chair, folded it over Sarah's shaking shoulders, and together they led her away to the little bedroom in back.

"When Hardy is through out there . . ." began Pete, looking with alarm at Sarah's paper-thin, colorless skin as she lay against the bedspread, but Connie was already in charge, replacing her own jacket with the afghan from the foot of the bed, sorting out the pillows.

"You go," she said to Pete. "Bring Hardy when he's through. Paul Roose left—you have to call Willy." And they looked at each other over Sarah's flattened form, for a minute nothing more between them than two minds thinking alike.

The police chief, Will McOwat, was an off-islander, brought down from Boston over Paul Roose's head to run the island's three-man force, and, as Connie had suspected, nobody in the living room seemed too anxious to get on the horn and shake him out. Instead the call went around and around the room for Paul Roose, who, as Connie had said, had already left. But before

Pete could get to the phone to call his friend Willy, the rescue wagon arrived, and the police chief's considerable height and weight at the head of the stretcher forged a path to Newby.

"Dead," Hardy said to the chief, and he went on to say other things—things about high velocity and single large-caliber projectiles and inversion of entry wound and eversion of exit wound edges, but it seemed that from Hardy's first word, *dead,* a magical kind of order descended over the room. Willy waved the stretcher crew back. He sent Ted Ball, the youngest, newest member of the force, to radio for Paul Roose. He sent Jerry Beggs to remove the remaining guests to a distant room, then bent his hulking body down to examine the twin wounds in Newby's skull.

Pete brought Hardy Rogers back to the little room to check on Sarah. The doctor folded himself into the tiny caned chair beside Sarah's bed, and Pete and Connie retreated a tactful distance as he poked around.

"She's doing a damned sight better than Newby," said Hardy finally, and Pete winced.

"I don't want you staying here alone tonight, Sarah," said Hardy.

"Nonsense." Sarah squeezed her eyes shut, a trick she was known to use to block the doctor out.

"I'll stay," said Connie.

"No," said Pete. "I'll be around. Why don't you go home?"

Connie gave him a look that he could no longer read, picked up her jacket from the back of the chair and left the room. Pete could hear her full, clear voice answering the police chief as he waylaid her with questions. There had been a time when the chief had shown some interest in Connie, but suddenly his interest had waned. Pete didn't think it was because of anything he'd said.

Pete sat and talked to Sarah in an effort to keep the sounds from the other room at bay, sounds of questions and answers, banging doors, retreating cars, moving furniture, clicking cameras, and, finally, Newby's body being carted away. He talked about nothing, but all the time his eyes strained through the half-dark at the old lady in the bed.

They went back a long way. Sarah Abrew had been one of the first customers of Factotum, the odd-job company Pete had started when he was sixteen and faced with leaving the island in search of a summer job. He'd almost done it, too—had almost walked the plank and become a Hooker, as they called it on Nashtoba when someone crossed the wooden causeway that separated the island of Nashtoba from the more commercially oriented, economically sound Cape Hook. But Pete hadn't been able to do it. Instead, he'd hung a sign on the bulletin board of Beston's Store, using a word off a recent vocabulary list, complete with definition: FACTOTUM, PERSON EMPLOYED TO DO ALL KINDS OF WORK.

First Sarah Abrew, eyesight failing, had hired him to read her the morning paper, and soon plenty of others had hired him to do plenty else. Mow lawns. Give surfing lessons. Pick up Uncle Al at the airport. Feed the pigs. Twenty years later Factotum was flourishing and Pete was still reading to Sarah despite the occasional set-to, such as her insistence on continuing to pay him or his insistence on divorcing his wife.

Pete stopped talking. Sarah's eyes were screwed less tightly shut and her chest movements had slowed. She was asleep, but Pete continued to sit there, now thinking about Newby. Against his will, he reenvisioned the mistletoe scene he had witnessed through the window. Congenial, Pete had called him, but weren't there situations where congeniality could be carried too far? Pete closed his eyes to clear his mind of the unwelcome image, and when he opened them again, Sarah was peering at him from her bed, her blue eyes sharp as a bird's.

"Go home."

"I'm in no . . ."

"Go home."

Pete went up to the bed, leaned over, and kissed Sarah's cheek. Sarah let go of the afghan and squeezed his hand. Pete left, but got only as far as the living room.

Two of the three policemen stood motionless in the center of Sarah's previously tidy room, its contents now either absent or awry.

"We can't find it," said Ted, his short red hair damp around the edges, his twenty-three-year-old cheeks very pink, his eyes tragic.

"Can't find *what?*" asked Pete.

Paul Roose's mouth twisted. He walked over to the window, where the spiderweb of cracks still gleamed, and peered at the hole in its center.

The outside door opened and closed and Willy reentered the room, his forehead glistening from either rain or perspiration.

"Can't find what?" Pete repeated.

Paul Roose suddenly turned and began to straighten up the room.

"Can't find *what?*"

"The bullet," said the chief. "It went into Newby, came out of Newby, and disappeared. What the hell are you doing?" This to Ted, who had joined Paul Roose in replacing Sarah's furniture. "Put that down. The bullet's here, and we don't leave till we find it. Let's go. Check those shelves. It could have lodged behind one of those. Check every knot in every piece of pine. Go over every inch of fabric on that couch."

The faces of the two policemen changed abruptly: Ted

10

Ball's filled with renewed youthful fervor and Paul Roose's went completely blank.

Pete began to leave the room.

"Hey," said Willy.

Pete stopped.

"*You* can take apart the tree."

Chapter
2

Connie Bartholomew got up very early the next morning, for no other reason than she figured it made just as much sense to be awake upright as it did to be awake lying down. She couldn't stop thinking about it, couldn't stop seeing it—first silly old Newby carrying on like that and Connie pretending she thought he was funny out of politeness, a new and uncomfortable personality trait she had recently tried on.

Then she'd heard it—that sound, that crack. She'd heard the crack of the glass first and had seen Pete's face behind that web of cracks second, as if the bullet had passed right between his eyes, as if he were shot dead and had already come back as some vengeful ghost to haunt her! And even with Newby crumpled dead at her feet, all she had been able to think was *Oh, my God, I've lost Pete*.

Connie allowed herself a short, bitter burst of laughter. As if she could lose him any more than she had already lost him! As if every time she saw him he didn't run like mad for the nearest door. Or the nearest *bush*.

Just like that she was seeing it yet again—the hole in the glass and Pete's face behind it.

She spent too much time in the shower and too little in front of the mirror, pulled on a clean pair of jeans and a turtleneck sweater, and jumped into her battered and beaten TR-6 to head for Sarah's.

She hadn't wanted to leave last night—hadn't, to tell the truth, wanted to be alone herself—but Pete hadn't seemed to want her to hang around. So what else was new? But at least she could get there bright and early this morning to make sure Sarah got up okay, to make sure she didn't want for anything that just maybe only Connie could do.

The truth was, Sarah Abrew was probably the only person in the world who loved Connie unconditionally, who, unlike some others she could name, had never slammed the door behind her the minute she had run.

Run. Yes, she had run. In a stupid, silly, desperate panic over Pete's contentment she had run, and although they had both been at fault before she ran, Connie knew that in Pete's mind the big fault, the San Andreas of faults, was hers and hers alone. She had run. Without warning, without explanation, and with another man. Pete's divorce papers came faster than Reno's. That *should* have been that. So why had she come back? Why had she accepted this teaching job that would keep her here through *June*? What had she thought would happen? She had said she was sorry. She had tried her best to explain something she herself didn't understand. What else was she supposed to do? She didn't know. All she knew was that now it was up to Pete—Pete, who now seemed bent on doing some running of his own.

"Why don't you go home," he'd said.

The police chief's Scout and the island's only cruiser were still parked in front of Sarah's house. Despite the lateness of the night before, Sarah was up and waiting,

13

perched in her favorite Victorian chair, her feet barely reaching the rug where Newby had fallen, the top of her short white hair coming to rest far below the thronelike spikes of the chair's back.

"They can't find the bullet," she said before Connie had even settled onto her couch. "Pete just left. Paul and Ted are still out in those woods. They spent half the night looking for the bullet. They just put my room back to rights, and they *still* can't find it. Now the chief's traipsing door-to-door asking anyone if they saw anything odd."

Anyone could be a very all-encompassing term, but then again, on this island, so could the word *odd*. Not for the first time, Connie felt a little sorry for the chief as Sarah's mouth tightened into a disapproving line that Connie had run into before, unconditional love or not. "I've a notion that chief's going to be as stubborn as you and Pete."

Connie opened her mouth to counter that old, familiar attack, but as she looked at Sarah she saw her slump down in her chair with the first signs of fatigue.

"They *shot* him. In *my home*. Newby Dillingham, who'd never hurt a fly."

Connie, who had been trying very hard for the past twenty-four hours not to think about Newby at all, answered simply, "I know."

Sarah abruptly straightened her spine. "I *told* you something like this was bound to happen the minute you let in those fool condominiums!"

"He wasn't letting in any condominiums, Sarah. As a matter of fact, maybe this happened because he was trying to keep them out. Half a million dollars is a lot of money. Maybe somebody—"

"Half a million dollars," repeated Sarah, with a sigh of disbelief. "And to think what the Peases must be saying now."

"The Peases?"

"The Peases. The *Peases*. They swapped that bait shop for the old farm up on the highway."

"The highway" was what Sarah Abrew called the cracked and sandy-shouldered old road that looped around the perimeter of the island, starting and ending at the causeway that connected Nashtoba to the rest of Cape Hook. Connie had forgotten that tidbit of island history—the Dillingham-Pease land swap—and suddenly it seemed like a tidbit worth remembering.

"When was that, Sarah?"

"Oh, not long ago." Sarah pressed her forehead as she thought and her skin crackled with fine lines. "Nineteen thirty-two, I think."

Connie looked at Sarah with affection, and a new kind of ease settled into her limbs. Maybe the time would come in Connie's own life when this one miserable year would shrink to insignificance among decades of peace. "That doesn't sound like a very fair swap, that run-down old farm for a piece of waterfront property."

"For a run-down old bait shop, you mean. That's all it was then; that's all it is now. Don't you forget, people didn't set such store by the waterfront back then. The farm was a going proposition and a fair deal at the time, leastways *most* people seemed to think so. But I don't know but what this half a million dollars'll just about kill Cyrus Pease."

Connie mulled that over. "Now that Ozzie's in control, do you think he'll sell?"

Sarah wrinkled up her nose in distaste and jabbed at the rug with her cane. "That old buzzard! It'd be just like him to do it to get my goat. Two hundred condominium units! There are eight hundred people on this island. This place is full up."

Connie, who was from New Jersey, was about to

15

laugh, but she changed her mind. Sometimes only one other person could make this island seem full up.

Sarah rubbed her temples wearily.

Connie was not one to wear out her welcome. She kissed Sarah good-bye and left.

Or almost. Once outside, Connie was herded into the police department's official all-terrain vehicle by the returning chief of police.

Will McOwat looked awful. His eyes were glazed, the skin below them hung in exhausted bags—even his great mass of muscle and bone seemed diminished by fatigue and strain. Connie secretly liked the unpopular police chief. Although he was soft-spoken, he talked straight. You could talk straight back. And despite the fact, or maybe because of the fact, that he was Pete's friend, Connie sensed he was in her corner.

"Any luck?" she asked.

At least he was still able to grin. "Nothing. Nobody admits to seeing anything or hearing anything, and even if they did, they sure aren't saying anything. The perfect row of monkeys—hear no evil, see no evil, speak no evil. Multiplied, of course."

"Wasn't anyone from the party any help? Wasn't Pete? He was right outside the whole time."

"No one inside was looking out. And Pete was looking in."

The police chief shot Connie a look just then that she decided to ignore.

"And I looked out," said Connie. "But not until after Newby was shot. I assume you're sure it was Newby they were after?"

The chief shook his head. "I assume nothing. I go by the book. Means, motive, opportunity. All we know at present is that the means was a high-powered rifle, and at this point all I can say is that anyone who wasn't at the party and had access to a high-powered rifle could have had the opportunity. But you're right—motive means nothing unless we're sure Newby Dillingham was the intended victim. But I'll tell you this. If that shot was meant for Newby Dillingham it was perfect, and I find it hard to argue with perfection. So I start with wondering who would want to kill Newby.''

And who *would* want to kill Newby? Connie wondered. Everyone already knew about the little problem between the brothers over the condos, but who besides Sarah had remembered about the Dillingham-Pease land deal? Connie told the chief about it.

She left right behind him, and she stayed behind him until he turned into Cyrus Pease's farm.

Rita Peck stamped the black mud off the stems of her gray heels and wondered why she bothered to deck herself out around this place. It wasn't as if she were in a real office managing a real corporation, after all. It wasn't even as if she couldn't do her job a whole lot better in jeans. Granted, she spent most of her day glued to the phone and ordering Factotum's crew around from the side of her mouth, but there were those occasional trips through the old, grungy piles of newspapers, and the wanderings through all the greasy lawn equipment in the halls, and then of course there had been that disgusting day when no one had been in and she'd had to catch all of Bill Pfiefer's chickens and put them back into their coop.

She shuddered, gave up on the shoes, pushed open Pete's front door, and walked into her little corner of Factotum, behind the desk and between the file cabinets.

There was a note on her desk from Pete. ''Am off for Jerry's barn.'' Rita mentally checked off Pete's whereabouts for the rest of the day and looked around for the other two members of Factotum's crew, not content until she had lined her ducks up in a row.

There was a splintering sound from the front door, as if the latch were going straight through the wood instead of sliding smoothly over it, and Rita didn't need to look up to know that Andy Oatley had arrived for work. *Pete* had hired Andy, Rita continually reminded herself, conveniently blocking from her mind a few of her own hirelings that had proved less than successful. Pete had been recovering from a knife wound when he hired the twenty-year-old Andy Oatley, and Rita knew that Andy's rippling musculature and youthful vigor had, at the time, greatly influenced the much weakened Pete in his decision to take him on. But Rita had a secret theory that the only reason Andy worked out so much was to discourage anyone who still insisted on calling him Annie Oakley. She had another theory that bulk such as Andy's was only an asset as long as it knew how to get out of its own way. Andy's definitely did not. He charged in now, whipping off his coat and the cup full of pens on Rita's desk in one fell swoop. Rita, knowing Andy by now, caught the cup and swatted at the coat just in time to save her left eyeball from a button.

"Sit!" she barked, and although Andy didn't sit, not having been completely trained as yet, he did stop moving.

"They can't find the bullet! I passed Pete on the road just now. He says they never found it inside, and they can't find where it left the house, either!"

Rita sniffed. How much would it have cost Pete to expand his note a sentence further so as to include a word about the bullet? Rita *hated* getting news thirdhand. She turned her back on Andy and snapped up the ringing phone. "Factotum." She added the rest of the business logo strictly for Andy's benefit, since he was now ambling toward the couch with the morning paper. "Person's employed to do all kinds of *work*."

Pete's second new-hire came through the door much

18

more quietly than the first. Rita often thought that just as she could psych out why Pete hired Andy, so she could see what must have attracted him to Allison Cox, daughter of the controversial new realtor, Nate Cox. Allison Cox was at the most five feet tall and about as big around as a fence post—not someone to whom you'd assign a moving job, say—but she had one clear asset in Rita's mind, and Rita could only hope it was an asset in Pete's as well. She was nothing whatsoever like his ex-wife.

"I'm sorry I'm late," said Allison, and right there was the first good example of what Rita meant. As far as she knew, Connie had never apologized for anything. Allison pulled off her watch cap and rumpled her still-wet hair into spikes. "My car wouldn't start and I had to wait for Dad to get back from Ozzie Dillingham's so he could drive me over here."

Rita watched Allison unbutton her coat and pull at the straps of her bib overalls. She was twenty-four, looked about twelve, and right at the moment she appeared irritatingly uninterested in passing on to Rita what her father and Ozzie had *said*. That wasn't much like Connie either. It was like pulling teeth to get Allison to speak, whereas Connie always blabbed out whatever she happened to be thinking at the moment, assuming she ever *thought* about anything at all.

"Is my check there?"

Rita pulled her own uncharitable thoughts up short and turned her mind back to the present. She opened her desk drawer, pulled out Factotum's checkbook, wrote out Allison's check, and handed it across. Almost as an afterthought, she wrote out Andy's as well.

"I'll be right back." Allison went outside.

Andy rose from the couch, peeked out the window, and waved frantically at Rita. "Check this out, will ya!"

Rita buckled her eyebrows. She did *not* approve of

spying. She got up, pulled down her skirt, and moved sedately to the window. Nate Cox sat in his rusting Chevy Impala, motor running, hand outstretched for Allison's check.

"Will you look at that! Second week in a row."

Rita returned to her desk and drummed her nails on the telephone. It was rumored that Nate Cox was not doing well in the real estate business, but was Nate Cox that desperate for ready cash that he had to commandeer his daughter's check? Rita looked at Allison's frayed overalls and thought, not for the first time, that there might have been another reason for Pete to have hired Allison Cox when plenty of others would have been more suited to Factotum's varied tasks.

But Nate Cox had just been at Ozzie Dillingham's, Allison said. What had the realtor said to Ozzie? More to the point, what had Ozzie said to the realtor? Now that Ozzie's brother was dead he could sell the bait shop. Would he? Rita pursed her lips at the bitter thought of hundreds of constantly running faucets draining away the island's precious aquifer, its single source of water. Didn't anyone care? Not Nate Cox. Nate Cox would make a bundle, use up the water, and leave the same way he had come. But Nate Cox wasn't the only one who would make a bundle off the condo deal. Ozzie Dillingham would make a bundle, too, wouldn't he? Rita wrinkled her nose at the thought of Ozzie. It occurred to her that island life would be a bit more pleasant if it had been *Ozzie* who'd been shot.

Rita gave a guilty shiver. Be fair. Who else would gain from condominiums on the harbor? Anyone in the business of making money off tourists would gain.

The phone rang again. The voice on the other end was encrusted with the telltale fog of a long-distance connection.

"Hello, Rita, this is Henry Long. We've decided to

come down earlier this year and I thought I'd better call ahead to make sure the cottage will be ready. Pete's supposed to install a bigger hot water heater and put in an outside shower.''

And that's the whole problem in a nutshell, thought Rita. Tourists. They get up in the morning and shower. They go for a swim and they shower again. They play tennis and they shower. They shower before they go out to eat.

Two hundred new condominium units. If only two people checked into each one, that would be half again the island's entire year-round population. Four hundred more people, two hundred more showers, running all the *time*.

Chapter
3

Beston's Store was Pete's first stop of the day. He walked across the worn and slanted floorboards of Beston's porch, empty of all hangers-on in the December chill, opened the door, and stepped into the double-barreled blast of the heat from the potbellied stove and the conversation from the old men seated around it.

"Sewage!" hollered Bert Barker. Bert was retired, or more accurately, supported by his wife's prime real estate on the Hook, and therefore frequently available for a winter cup of coffee around Beston's stove. "Sewage! What the Christ is a little sewage? The clams love it. I tell you, those condos'll be the best thing that ever happened to this island. Sewage! You think the locals don't shit?"

"They may very well do so," said Evan Spender, somewhat equivocally, Pete thought, "but the fact remains that they don't, as a rule, do it all together, in small confined spaces, only a few feet away from the water." Evan Spender was not as old as Bert, being in his late fifties at most, and he still worked as a telephone repairman, but not very visibly. He was more visible around Beston's stove in winter, on Beston's porch in summer, and, more recently, around Rita's desk at Factotum. Pete figured Evan's finding his way to Rita's desk was only another example of Evan's good-old-fashioned common sense. And so, some might say, was his remark about the sewage.

"Seems as though, what with all these hotshot young engineers running around these days, they could figure out how to deal with a little sewage," said Ed Healey. Ed Healey was also retired—from everything but drinking and eating, that is—and lived at Beston's as much as he did at home. He was obese, benevolent, alcoholic, and diplomatic. "That's not to say that I don't see the danger," he went on. "After all, modern science solves its problems a lot slower than it causes them, right?"

"Hi," said Pete.

Bert Barker kept right on hollering, not seeming to notice that he was switching sides as well as topics.

"Modern science! What did modern science ever do for you? Go talk to that lousy cop, why don't you? Do you think he's going to find out who shot Newby? Not on your life! Modern science! Paul Roose says he had them up all night looking for the lousy bullet, and did they find it? Nosiree. No bullet, no science, and that's all they hired him for, all this big-city, so-called science! You mark my words! He'll spend the next two months looking for some lousy bullet, some fingerprints, some damn-fool *scientific* evidence, when what we need is someone who'll just get out there and find out who did it! Why, Pete here'd be more likely to . . ."

"Finding out who did it is one thing," said Evan Spender. "Proving it in court is another. Unless you catch him doing it, you need those other things—fingerprints, bullets . . ."

"What the hell do you think I'm trying to say here?

23

Why didn't he catch him doing it—that's my point! There are only eight hundred people on this island. How hard could it be to—"

"It seems funny, though, doesn't it?" Pete cut in. "Not finding the bullet?"

Bert Barker opened his mouth and took a breath.

"Evan?" said Pete quickly. "Doesn't it seem funny to you?"

"Seeing as how it went through Newby pretty clean, maybe it went clear out the other side of the house," said Evan.

"They looked. They can't find any evidence that it left the room, or lodged in the wall or the furniture or anything."

Evan nodded. "So who's the chief got in mind?"

"Nobody yet, as far as I know," Pete answered, and then winced as Bert Barker tuned up once again.

"Nobody yet! Nobody yet! You mark my words, we'll be sitting here asking that same damned thing two months from now. They should've given the job to Paul Roose. They should've—"

"Heard the chief was out talking to Cyrus Pease," said Evan Spender, seemingly following some train of thought of his own.

"You *bet* he should talk to Cyrus Pease!" said Bert. "I can tell you this condo deal's going up old Cyrus's ass sideways. He's been pissing and moaning all over town for fifty years about that swap. I'll be damned if he wants to see those Dillinghams make one more red cent!"

Ed Healey shook his head. "But even Cyrus has to admit no one could have guessed that old bait shop'd go for a half a million dollars."

"Don't kid yourself," said Bert. "Cyrus'll tell you the Dillinghams guessed it back in 1932! He blames them for corn going bust right about then, doesn't he? He blames them for the tourists and the fishing picking up, for water property skyrocketing, right? He swears old man Dillingham knew what was coming when he made that swap. He's nursed his grudge this long, he'll blow his gasket over this new deal—you mark my words.''

"You never can tell with farming," began Evan, but Bert Barker charged back in.

"Farming! Who in his right mind would farm anyway? Too much work. Ask Cyrus—he doesn't do squat with that place anymore. *He* should sell out for condos.''

"Maybe he will," said Ed. "This half a million's got everyone's blood up. Heard that's why Abel Cobb came back—to put the old house on the market. I'm glad Colonel Cobb's not alive to see that.''

Pete felt a sudden depression descend on his spirits. The dignified, stately old Cobb place had been in the family for over a hundred fifty years, and Pete guessed Abel's father, the Colonel, wouldn't be the only Cobb rolling over in his grave at the thought of Abel selling out.

"Half a million for a bait shop!" said Bert, shaking his head in awe, or more likely, envy. "What do you figure Nate Cox is gonna clear on that?''

Pete frowned, thinking, not for the first time, of Allison Cox. As much as Pete would hate to see row after row of condominiums lining the unassuming little harbor, he suspected that such a sale would go far toward removing that cloud from Allison's eyes. Only last month Nate Cox had sold his house and moved his wife and daughter into the annex in back of the real estate office—not the kind of a move an up-and-coming realtor would be apt to make.

The men around the stove kept gossiping, but since Pete wasn't retired as yet, he bought his box of nails and moved on.

Jerry Beggs's barn was next on Pete's agenda. Pete

swung his truck along Shore Road, into the dirt drive that wandered past Jerry's three-story yellow Victorian house, and up to the half-framed barn in back.

Jerry Beggs ran the Bookworm Shop on Main Street and had gotten so caught up in the Christmas surge that he had had to turn to Factotum for help. Pete was signed on to help build the barn, Allison to help out in the shop. Pete liked Jerry. He also liked building Jerry's barn. Jerry's place was more inland than Pete's cottage on the marsh, tucked in cozily against the island's only white pine forest, making a change from the usual rough scrub pines that blanketed everything else. As Pete worked with Jerry in companionable silence the soft and graceful trees behind him seemed to talk to him in the Nashtoba winter wind, and that was one of the reasons, when Jerry had gotten too busy with the Christmas rush at the store to contribute much of his own time to the barn, Pete had elected to finish the barn alone. He had brought Andy one day and Andy had talked so much Pete could barely hear the trees.

Andy had also sawed off the toe of his sneaker.

Pete had worked doggedly alone. The framing would soon be done. Today, however, the conversation in the trees was overshadowed not by Andy but by the voices inside his own head.

What *was* Nate Cox's cut on half a million dollars, and where had he been the night of Sarah's party? Where had Ozzie Dillingham been that night, or Cyrus Pease? Just how steamed *was* Cyrus over the land swap and the condo offer?

Should he have said something to Connie last night?

At noon Pete ate a sandwich in the truck and climbed back up onto the roof. He only came down when Will McOwat pulled into the drive at dusk, looking to drag Pete off for a beer.

*   *   *

26

Pete picked up the Santa candle centered on the red and white tablecloth at Lupo's and looked into its coal-black eyes. It was one of the things Pete liked best about Christmas—things remained the same, year after year. Lupo's Santa candles, for example. The green vines Rita hung at Factotum. Sarah's party . . . Well, not Sarah's party. Not this year.

"Still no bullet?" Pete asked, as the beer Willy had just paid for was slid across the booth.

Willy shook his head. It was a long head, oval on top and squared off on the bottom, made even longer by the forehead that expanded as the hair withdrew. "We searched outside all day yesterday and today while the light lasted. No bullet, no cartridge case. No clues. We need the bullet. Eventually we want to match the weapon to the rifling marks on the bullet."

"The what?"

"You know. Lands and grooves. Every manufacturer varies the rifling and it leaves marks on the—"

"Lands and what?" Unlike Bert Barker, Pete had developed, through his association with the chief, a healthy respect for science.

"Grooves. Lands and grooves." The chief grabbed a pen out of his pocket, pulled a clean napkin off the nearest table, and began to draw a series of curved lines followed by something that looked like a sawed-off snowflake. "Spiral tracks are cut into the barrel of a rifle to propel the bullet out and to put a spin on it that keeps it from tumbling end over end. The troughs that are cut into the barrel are called the grooves. The raised ridges between the grooves are called the lands. Each manufacturer has his own pattern of rifling, and each individual barrel can have random scratches of its own that will affect the bullet. When the bullet passes through the rifle, the lands and grooves and scratches leave their marks on a bullet just like a signature. If we get the gun

27

and the bullet we can match them to each other without a doubt." Willy sighed. "*If* we get the bullet. Which we've got to do." He siphoned off more beer. "*If* we had the bullet, or even if we could pinpoint where it exited the house, we'd be able to plot its trajectory and narrow down where it came from, maybe find a cartridge casing. The casing would help. It could tell us caliber and maybe something about the weapon itself. The casing gets marked up as it gets ejected from the gun. As it is, not knowing just where the bullet came from, we're hunting blind."

"I can tell you where the bullet came from," said Pete. "It came from behind me. And it wasn't above me by enough—I can tell you that, too! If I hadn't ducked when I did . . ." And against his will Pete saw again the vivid image that had driven him down into the bushes: Newby's stupid mistletoe trick and Connie's face, laughing. He lowered his beer by half an inch, sighed, pushed it away, and looked at the chief, who was still looking down at his drawing, his expression a trifle miffed.

"So tell me who did it, okay?"

It was no joke. Nobody on Nashtoba opened up freely to this off-island chief, and because he was off-island he lacked much of the background knowledge the rest of them took for granted. Pete's feelings about science notwithstanding, he knew there was much to Bert Barker's way of thinking. The island was small, and its inhabitants were open enough, among themselves, that secrets didn't stay secret long. In theory it should be easy enough to find out who might have wanted to kill Newby, providing, of course, that you were *inside* the rumor mill, not out. Paul Roose would be the chief's logical source of information, but Paul Roose's nose was so out of joint over being passed over for the job as chief that it was, as Willy once said, "like pulling teeth to get him to cough up directions to the john." So although Pete's friendship with the police chief was based in part on mutual loneliness, there was also another layer beneath the beers at Lupo's: the chief needed the inside information that Pete, an island native, possessed, and Pete, an island native, felt a protective instinct to keep tabs on what the chief was thinking.

And about whom.

"So tell me about the Dillinghams."

"The Dillinghams. They never got along to start with, but this condominium thing's made it worse than ever."

"Ever hear it go as far as threats?"

Pete stopped to think. The only out-and-out threats he remembered hearing of late were the usual ones between Rita and her daughter, Maxine, heard from his usual spot, smack in the middle of the two of them. "Threats, no," said Pete, "but it's gotten the whole island formed up into pro and con contingents. Everyone's starting to dig in their heels and things have been getting a little heated here and there."

"Here and where?"

Pete shrugged. "Anywhere. Beston's porch. The post office. Here." He turned around and looked behind him, but the row of fireplug-shaped backsides at the bar didn't seem too animated tonight. Even the bartender, Dave Snow, seemed bored.

The chief seemed to mull over the Dillingham situation through the next third of his beer. He had done his homework, it seemed. "Newby had no close family, other than his brother. He never made a will. So Ozzie inherits by default, the sale could go through."

Pete paused, considering the idea of Ozzie as killer, and was surprised to find the concept plausible enough. The problem seemed to lie more with the idea of Newby as *victim*. Condos or not, Pete had a hard time believing that anyone would intentionally harm Newby, especially his own brother, even if that brother was Ozzie. For some reason just then the image of Newby's mistletoe trick flashed at Pete once again.

"So where was Ozzie Saturday night?"

"Home alone."

Pete considered. "Isn't that a pretty good alibi right there? If you were the murderer wouldn't you at least try to make something up?"

The chief didn't answer.

Pete decided it was time to cash in on his part of this deal. "So you've been talking to Cyrus Pease?"

The chief shook his head, still amazed, Pete knew, at the speed and efficiency of the island rumor mill. "I've been talking to Cyrus Pease. He hasn't been talking back much. He confirmed the land swap with the Dillinghams—that's about it. And I talked to his neighbors, the Waxmans." The chief shook his head again. "That Evelyn Waxman. I get nothing out of her, she gets my signature on her petition and ten bucks for the cookies and punch for the Christmas party at school."

Pete grinned. "But couldn't this shooting have been an accident?"

"It was a dead aim and a clean shot, right to the temple. At night. What kind of an accident would you call that?"

A very lucky one, thought Pete. Or a very *un*lucky one, if you happened to be Newby, of course.

By the time Pete pulled up to the little cottage on the marsh the darkness outside was complete and Rita was long gone, with only a single light burning to welcome him home. He looked at the different blacknesses around him—the faintly luminous black of the sky, the deeper black of the sea below it, the deepest black of the marsh stretching from the water to the edge of his stubbly lawn. He looked again at the yellowed square of window below the steeply angled cottage roof, and just like that he was seeing it again—another lit window, Newby, the mistletoe, and Connie's face, laughing. What had happened then? He had heard the smack as the bullet hit the glass, had seen the cracked window empty as Newby hit the floor and the guests pulled away. . . .

Pete pushed open his own living room door and smiled at the sprig of holly Rita had stuck in the cup that held her pens. One Christmas Eve Connie had stuck it in her teeth and . . . Pete stopped smiling. What were the odds of Connie being around for Christmas this year? Pretty slim. But okay—hadn't he gotten through last year all right without her? Pete's parents had come from Florida as usual, Pete's sister, Polly, had come from Maine—Christmas had still been Christmas, hadn't it? True, his parents had spent the whole time trying to pretend Connie never existed, and true, Polly had spent two hours every day trying to get Pete to talk about What Went Wrong, and true, Pete had finally gotten drunk and stayed that way.

The phone on Rita's desk rang, and Pete snatched it up. "Hello."

"Whew!" said a distant voice on the other end of the line. "Who were you expecting? You sound a little out of sorts."

"Hi, Dad," said Pete, and he relaxed onto the edge of the desk, his back to the holly, his mind suddenly and gratefully wiped clean of Connie.

"Listen, your mother and I were talking, and we had an idea about this Christmas—that maybe this year you'd like to come on down here instead. This retirement group here is having a party, and we thought you and your sister hadn't been down in a while, maybe you'd feel like being someplace warm for a change."

When Pete didn't answer, his father pushed on.

"We're getting old, Pete. The cold is colder than it once was, know what I mean?" And his father laughed that hearty laugh that meant many things but never what it said it meant. "Here," he said at once, before Pete could answer. "Your mother wants to say hello. Come say hello to Pete, Lou."

"Hi, dear!"

"Hi, Mom."

"What do you think, dear? Of course I know how you are about tradition, but your father thinks . . . What? What?" This to the land beyond the phone where his father lived more comfortably, communicating his most intimate questions from secondhand. "No, Ralph, he hasn't said yes. Well, he hasn't said no, either! Peter, really, you don't have to answer now . . . What? What? Oh! Yes. Your father says he'll send you the ticket."

"I can buy my own ticket," said Pete, his teeth beginning to clench.

"He's buying a ticket! Ralph, he's . . ."

"I didn't *say* that, Mom. I said I *could* buy my own ticket. I can *afford* a ticket to Florida. It's just a matter of . . ." Of what? Of hating pink houses? Of loving the grizzle and gray of Nashtoba at Christmas?

"Is it hot there?" he asked lamely.

"Eighty-two today."

Eighty-two. Pete wrinkled his nose in distaste, hedged some more with his mother, and finally wormed his way off the phone. He wasn't going to spend Christmas in any eighty-two degree, palmy, pink retirement place. He yanked Rita's holly out of its holder and threw it in the wastebasket, thinking as he watched it flutter down that it looked a hell of a lot more like mistletoe than Newby's stupid philodendron leaf did, and just like that, there it was again before his eyes—the leaf, the laugh, the bullet.

But *where* was the bullet? Pete wandered down the

hall to the part of Factotum that housed his cramped living quarters, trying to distract himself by concentrating on the missing bullet. If what the chief said was true, they would have to find the bullet so they could match it to the gun, to match the killing of Newby to the owner of the gun, no matter what other evidence, short of confession, they came across along the way. Pete walked down the hall past the rooms that he and Connie had once lived in but that had now all been subtly confiscated by Factotum, into the two remaining rooms where he now lived—a kitchen/dining room and a bedroom/living area.

Connie had taken little with her. Pete flopped down on the bed and looked at the pair of rocking chairs that had been Connie's particular treasures. He looked at the ceiling, trying to force his mind to go another way, but even as he did so he could at the same time stand back from it and watch it as it wandered down a path of its own.

The bullet. The window. Newby kissing Connie. *Connie* kissing *Newby*. Eject!

It was no use. He couldn't stop recreating the scene through the window again: Connie's tall, strong bones, her wholesome flesh, her face tipped back in the light as Newby kissed her, the next minute the window empty of everything but Sarah's stark, old-fashioned chairs. Yes, that pretty well summed it all up—Connie there one minute and gone the next, with nothing left to show for it but a couple of chairs.

Chairs. Suddenly Pete sat up, seeing those chairs at Sarah's clearly for the first time. He had seen them once, the way they had looked from outside the window. He had seen them again when he helped the police search the room.

Pete carefully reviewed his memory bank. He combed

33

Sally Gunning

through it for every scene from Sarah's party, beginning
to end, room to room, person to person, chair to chair.
  Yes.
  It was possible.
  It was more than possible.
  He might just know where that bullet was.

Chapter
4

Connie lay on the couch with a paperback copy of *Great Expectations* in one hand and a Ballantine Ale in the other, making use of neither. The book she had found in Pete's truck, and although she had at first snorted with derision at the sight of it, she had later gone back and stolen it.

Great Expectations. That was Pete all over. She snapped the book shut, this time with *self*-derision, and closed her eyes. So what was the point? She'd flown the coop. He'd slammed the door after her. The whys and wherefores were of no concern anymore, the fact that she had come back apparently of no interest.

There was a knock at the door, and Connie shot up off the couch, startled, simultaneously looking at the clock as she landed on her feet.

It was nine o'clock at night. Connie wasn't expecting anybody at nine o'clock at night, not on Nashtoba, and of all the people she wasn't expecting, Peter Bartholomew was the one she was expecting least.

"I'm sorry it's so late," he said, but he didn't seem to really mean it, didn't even seem to expect her to mind it. Connie stepped back further on her side of the doorjamb and stared across it at Pete.

What was it about him that was different? Or was she stopping in her tracks because of all there was about him that was suddenly the same? She knew him so well in so many ways. She knew that cowlick that he seldom bothered to fight down, she knew the long, lean muscles he had acquired, not from working out but from just plain working hard. She knew that wool baseball jacket! She knew those worn but stiffly clean jeans, right down to the spot rubbed white on the bottom of the pocket from the loose change that accumulated there.

Connie stood there dumbly, not knowing what to say, for once in her life not trying to say it anyway.

"Could I see your jacket?" asked Pete, not seeming to notice (or to care?) that Connie was standing there stupefied at the sight of him.

"Jacket?"

"The leather jacket. It was hanging over the back of the chair, right behind Newby. I remember seeing it through the window. Later you put it around Sarah, and then when you left her bedroom you wore it home."

"Jacket?" Connie said again, alarmed at the wave of disappointment that washed over her. He was here to look at her *jacket?*

"It's the only place the bullet could be," he repeated patiently, and suddenly Connie was with him. The bullet! She turned, charging up the stairs with Pete still babbling behind her.

"They took apart Sarah's house but couldn't find the bullet. There's nowhere else it could logically be except your jacket. It went through a window and in and out of Newby's skull; it must have been pretty spent by the time it hit your jacket."

"It's leather," said Connie, as she pulled it off the hook on the wall. Pete grabbed for it before she could even feel the pockets. "It's leather. It's heavy, thick. It's . . ."

He didn't seem to be listening. He felt all over the jacket, concentrating on the lumpy bottom edge where the leather of the coat joined up with the synthetic lining, and then he looked up at her and grinned with a grin that was such a long-lost friend she almost felt like crying.

"Here!" Pete poked a finger through a rip in the lining that hadn't been there when Connie first set out for Sarah's, she was sure, and then he fished around inside the jacket's bottom edge. "And here!" Out of the rip he pulled a coppery-looking slug of metal that seemed insultingly insignificant, considering that it had killed a man.

"Oh, God," said Connie.

"We'd better find Willy."

Was it finding the bullet or was it that casual assumption of the "we" of the thing that finally set Connie off smiling too? For just a minute they stood there grinning at each other like idiots. For just a minute it was like it had been so briefly in Sarah's bedroom the night Newby was killed, the two of them together and no baggage in between. Then Connie remembered that Pete was surely grinning over the bullet, that he had only come here over the bullet, that the light in his eye was only the light of a mystery freak who had uncovered a clue. She stopped smiling. Pete stopped smiling. They looked away. Still, Pete assumed she was coming with him, and Connie went.

They found Will McOwat at home. Connie had never been to the police chief's home before and was shocked to see how impermanent his surroundings appeared. There were no pictures on the bare white walls; what furniture he had was necessary, not decorative; and unpacked boxes, not books, were piled up on the shelves. Was he planning on getting fired?

Once Pete showed him the bullet and told the bizarre tale, the chief began to lay out plans—plans that included her, plans that would bring the three of them back to Sarah's to recreate the exact positions of the parties present at the shooting.

"Wait a minute," said Connie, looking at the clock. "It's nine thirty. You're going to Sarah's *now?* This is Nashtoba you're talking about. This is the middle of the night around here."

The chief looked from Connie to Pete and then gave Pete a funny, raised-eyebrow kind of look that made Connie mad and drove Pete to say, "I'll call Sarah now," just, Connie suspected, so he could leave the room.

"Well, you don't need me." Connie headed for the door and then remembered that she'd ridden to the chief's in Pete's truck.

"We need you all right. You were standing with Newby and we need all the key persons who were involved in the scene at the time."

"So who's going to hold up Newby?"

The chief grinned.

Pete, who had just returned, didn't. "Sarah's up and ready," he said.

Connie had to give in. If Sarah could take it, who was she to wimp out?

The chief left the room, and Pete, who had hardly stopped talking since the goddamned bullet first appeared, suddenly had nothing to say now that he found himself alone with Connie. They stood there side by side and silent until Willy returned with a small, sturdy box in which he carefully packed his treasured bullet and shoved it into his coat. "I have to stop at the station first. Follow me."

It was a long, quiet ride. At the station Pete followed the chief inside, clearly not wishing to be left behind with Connie, and Connie followed the two of them, not feeling like waiting around on just anyone's whim. The chief taped shut the box with the bullet and locked it in the safe. Then he collected various strange-looking instruments and folders and tapes as he filled in Ted Ball, who was manning the desk. "We're going to Abrew's. I want you to track down Paul and send him over as soon as you can."

It was an even longer, quieter ride to Sarah's. Connie's mind drifted away, watching the dark shadows of the scrub pines fly by the windows. This island. It was small, flat, mildewed and gray, barely connected to the world by an unreliable row of planks that washed out with every storm. Didn't anyone understand just what it had cost her to come back? She looked sideways at Pete, practically crawling up the door handle of his truck to keep away, refusing to look her in the eye.

Suddenly Connie felt very tired.

It was that much more irritating to find the eighty-six-year-old Sarah Abrew perched in her chair, chipper and alert, remaining so throughout the whole ordeal.

Connie went through the motions as if she were in a trance, moving without argument when the chief beckoned to her, hanging her jacket on the ladder-backed chair, where, to the best of her knowledge, it had hung at Sarah's party.

Paul Roose arrived. He walked around Connie's jacket twice. He examined the lining and felt the thickness of the leather as the chief watched. He pushed the freely hanging jacket back and forth. "That'd do it," he said.

"Do what?" asked Pete, miraculously regaining his tongue.

Paul's mouth twisted in a half grimace, half grin.

"Took the wind right out of it. Thirty caliber, fully jacketed. These things just keep on going as a rule."

"Fully what?" asked Pete.

Paul looked at the chief, but the chief only squinted back at him. He went on. "Jacketed. It means the bullet is covered with copper so it doesn't disintegrate. But the leather coat was hanging loosely from the chair so it could move with the force of the bullet, absorbing the impact. It stopped it cold." He shook his head.

The chief squinted hard at Paul. "Let's go."

Pete was the first to move—away from Connie, of course. He went outside and soon he reappeared in the window, looking miles away, his pale face framed by Sarah's ridiculous, flickering lights.

They began.

Pete waved from the window. The chief pushed and prodded first the chair, and then Connie and Paul Roose, the stand-in for Newby, until everyone was lined up just how Pete and Connie remembered it.

Pete came back in.

Connie started to move but Willy stopped her. Tapes came out, measurements were taken, this time Willy went out into the night, and of course Pete at once began to talk to Paul Roose.

"This business of the bullet being thirty caliber, does it mean much?"

"Yep."

"Why?"

"They aren't legal for hunting, not around here."

"Why not?"

Paul waved at the window. "We're too populated. The bullets travel too far. You need real woods to hunt with something that large."

"So firing that bullet was against the law?"

Connie snorted. "And here I thought killing Newby was legal."

40

From her chair in the corner Sarah Abrew cackled. Paul Roose grinned. Pete looked away. So what did he do, throw out his sense of humor along with the marriage license? Suddenly Connie was so inexplicably tired she felt she would drop.

"So who'd use thirty-caliber bullets?"

Paul Roose shrugged. "Guys who hunt large game. It's legal up north. Guys who match shoot, target shoot." He looked at the jacket on the chair, then out the window, and then off into the night. "Whoever did this shoots a bit, I'd say."

Connie swayed on her feet. Pete, apparently catching the movement out of the corner of his eye, looked at her in surprise. She could feel the skin on her face stretched taut with the strain of this weird exhaustion.

"Hey," said Pete. "Connie's had it. Let me take her home."

Willy looked reluctant.

Pete persisted. "Come on," he said to Connie. "I'll run you home."

Connie followed him out.

They didn't speak on that ride either, but somehow it wasn't the same.

Chapter
5

Pete spent a restless night haunted by ghosts of Christmases past—ghosts that all had Connie's eyes, ghosts that never said anything but seemed to mean different things by the different silences, ghosts that cried out to him to *say* something, to *do* something, to *act*, but by saying what? *Doing* what? Doing it *when?* The next morning he shaved, showered, dressed, ate his Wheaties, and exited his kitchen into the rest of Factotum, still trying unsuccessfully to make sense of his life and his dreams.

Rita Peck was already at her desk, and at first glance she was her usual pleasant and well-appointed self. Her jet-black hair, cut in a short bob, moved when she moved and yet never sent a single gleaming hair out of place. Her shoes matched her belt, her blouse blended with her skirt, her figure fleshed out her clothes with no room left over for wrinkles or gaps.

"Good morning!" said Rita brightly, shaking out the morning paper.

Pete looked at her a second time, noted the perfect

posture, and began to wonder what was wrong. "Good morning," he said.

"So you found the bullet last night."

Was that it? The fact that he'd neglected to call her about the bullet last night? Rita hated to get news secondhand.

"The chief called," she went on. "He wants you to stop by."

Maybe that was it. Pete sometimes spent a lot of Factotum's time with the chief.

The paper cracked again, Rita smiled again. "So! Did you get Connie home all right?"

Bingo.

Rita Peck was forty-two years old to Pete's thirty-six. Somewhere in the course of the many years of their friendship Rita had translated those extra six years into a full license for mothering, and whereas ordinarily Pete found Rita's fussing mildly amusing, he was annoyed by it today. Last night's silent ride home with Connie had unsettled him, and before he could sort out what was so unsettling about it Rita was reminding him that she could not forgive Connie for leaving. Somehow he didn't feel like being reminded of that today.

"I'll stop by the station now," he said.

But Rita had other things in mind. First Pete had to load the newly split wood into his truck, a job that would have gone more smoothly if Rita hadn't sent Andy and Allison out to help. Since Andy's throw was highly erratic Pete spent a good part of the time ducking, but still, he found Andy a lot less disconcerting than Allison. She was always silently popping up in front of him when he was sure she was far behind him, and every time he spoke to her in passing she looked at him with quiet gray eyes and scurried away without saying a word.

Then he had to deliver the cordwood to Art Keiley. Art Keiley lived near the causeway that connected Nashtoba to Cape Hook, a place that was always somewhat symbolic for Pete. Today the water between island and mainland was spiked with rickracks of foam. Pete got out of the truck and faced directly into the blow with that warped sense of satisfaction he always felt when he was standing on the island side of the causeway. On this side the trees were stunted scrub, the marsh grass flat and brown, the wind wet and bitter. On the other side there were milder winds, taller trees, more colorful grasses. Pete liked this side best.

He turned his back to the wind. Coming down the sand-covered tar road was Art Keiley's gray head bobbing above a royal blue jogging suit. His sneakers had reflectors on the rims and in each hand he held a barbell-shaped five-pound weight that he swung up and down with exaggerated movements. He puffed into the drive and up to Pete, looking over the truckbed at the pile of wood.

"Power walking," he explained. "Since I retired I do five miles a day. I hear when the condos go in they're going to have a health club, a real spa, someplace I can really work out."

"What condos?" Pete asked innocently.

Art Keiley squinted at Pete and wisely changed the subject. "Just stack the wood over there." He pointed to a spot next to the garage. "I have three and a half more miles to go." He puffed off down the road.

Pete was still heaving his five-pound logs into neatly stacked piles when Art Keiley puffed back in.

Pete's next stop was the bank. The Nashtoba Seamen's Savings Bank looked like everything else on the

44

island from the outside—all white clapboards and twelve-over-twelve windows—but inside the realities of modern-day banking took hold: steel vaults, barred gates, the bank officers hermetically sealed behind what was probably bulletproof glass. Pete looked through the mortgage officer's windowpane and decided he was just as glad that particular office wasn't open to the crowd. The realtor Nate Cox leaned over the mortgage officer's desk, arms flying, face burning, mouth spluttering. The mortgage officer shook his head once, twice, three times. Nate Cox continued to rail. The mortgage officer picked up some papers from his desk and slid them tentatively under Nate's nose, but the realtor swatted them away. The mortgage officer rose from his desk, walked to the door, and opened it. He spoke with that calm regret peculiar to mortgage officers and undertakers alone. "I'm sorry, Mr. Cox."

Nate Cox barged past Pete and out the door.

Pete felt uneasy as Nate Cox sped away. The realtor may not have been on the island long, but he had been here long enough for Pete to sense a dramatic change in him. There was a new aggression in him that was not going to do any better and was, in fact, doomed to do far worse with the island's take-things-as-they-come population.

When Pete finally strolled into the station things didn't look too urgent, if Paul Roose's casual pose as he leaned over the counter talking to the dispatcher, Jean Martell, was any indication.

"Here he is!" Jean hollered into the hall as she spied Pete, and then, to Pete: "Chief wants you." Jean liked to keep in charge of things. It was almost impossible to slip by her post at the desk without revealing to her everything you knew. Conversely, it was as hard to slip

45

by the desk without Jean revealing to you everything *she* knew.

"Well, here I am."

"Well, wait one minute. He's on the phone with the forensics lab again. He's already driven all the way up there this morning with the bullet. I hear Nate Cox has been over to Ozzie's already. What's Ozzie going to do?"

Paul Roose twitched one corner of his mouth into something slightly less, or possibly slightly more, than his usual cryptic grin. Jean Martell and her husband, Alton, owned an Italian restaurant, Martelli's, not far from Ozzie's bait shop, and Jean and Alton made no secret of their enthusiasm for the CRAP project. For that matter, neither did Paul, although just what he stood to gain out of it other than more work policing the premises, Pete didn't know.

"No idea," Pete answered her.

"Heard a while ago he was thinking of selling the boats, leaving Newby with the shop, going to Florida and trying his luck down there. Now he can sell the bait shop *and* the boats and not work for the rest of his life!"

Pete thought of the retired Art Keiley, tearing around with his weights all day. Is that what *he* had wanted—not to work for the rest of his life? And what about Paul Roose? Paul was nearing retirement age. Once Will McOwat arrived from Boston to take charge, Paul had faded into the woodwork of island life, doing what he had to do and precious little more. Was he also waiting for the day when he wouldn't have to do anything at all?

Pete turned to Paul. "Do we know anything new after last night?"

Paul Roose peered thoughtfully at Pete before answering. "My guess'd be the shot came from uphill, from around a hundred yards away. Accuracy of the shot, behavior of the bullet, trajectory, shot being at night and all.''

From down the hall a door creaked. At once Jean moved back toward the desk and Paul glided like a long shadow through the door to his immediate right, conspirators in the face of the enemy.

Willy McOwat beckoned to Pete from the end of the hall. As Pete walked by he saw Paul Roose with an oily rag in his hand, leaning over a table covered with a variety of tubular and knobby metal parts that could only come from guns.

''Housecleaning?'' Pete asked the chief, nodding over his shoulder toward Paul.

''Housecleaning. Yeah.''

''Despite a murder investigation or because of it?''

The chief ignored him. ''So what about it? Know anyone who hunts big game?''

Pete shook his head, thinking of Hemingway and lions and elephants and poor old Francis Macomber.

''Bear. Moose. Deer.''

Pete returned to the continental United States, but still he had to shake his head.

''Vermont? Maine?''

Pete could call to mind only his own sister, Polly, who was now living in Maine and who might or might not be going to Florida for Christmas.

Christmas.

Connie.

''Where are you going for Christmas, Will?''

''Sister's. Connecticut. How about local marksmen? Target shoots, match shoots, things like that?''

''This isn't much of a gun place,'' Pete answered, and then, remembering the room he had just passed, he added, ''except for the police station, of course.''

Willy didn't seem to care much for that answer, but at least he gave up with the questions.

Before Pete returned to Jerry's barn he decided to swing down Shore Road by the old Pease farm. It had started to rain now, and the sand that blew continually over the road stuck to his wet tires and smacked into the bottom of his truck. The scrub pines and bare beach plum bushes turned from gray to black in the wet, and the wind was as raw and as cold as wind could get, but as he pulled into sight of the Pease property he saw Cyrus out in the field driving in a post.

The Pease farm was old—very old. Pete couldn't remember Nashtoba without it, and he doubted that even the eighty-six-year-old Sarah Abrew could, but both he and Sarah could remember when it was bigger. The sloping pasture and the white clapboard house and barn rode the shallow hill as if they had always belonged, but topping the rise was something that didn't look quite so in keeping with the scene. The Waxman house, a modernized version of an old Cape with attached garage and enlarged windows, perched on the land the Peases had had to sell to make ends meet.

Pete scrambled out of the truck, zipped his jacket against the weather, and trekked through the mud to Cyrus. Maybe it was the weather, or maybe it was the recalcitrant post, or maybe it was the seventy-odd years of creases that had eaten into Cyrus's face, but as Pete approached he thought he had seldom seen anyone who looked so out of sorts.

"Need a hand?"

Cyrus didn't answer, but that didn't mean anything one way or the other. Pete leaned into the post, correcting its angle as Cyrus swung. After two more swings Cyrus handed over the sledgehammer and Pete tapped the post in nice and straight.

"Hard work, Cyrus."

Cyrus Pease wiped the dirt off his hands and onto his dungarees. "What isn't?"

"I dunno. Selling out?"

Cyrus Pease leaned into the rain and looked off toward the Waxmans'. There was no warm, neighborly welcome in his eye. "You think selling out isn't hard? You think this rotten piece of rock-filled hill means nothing to me but money? Money's here today and gone tomorrow. What matters is land. Once that's gone, there's no getting it back." Maybe it was Pete's imagination, but it seemed to him that Cyrus's rock-hard gaze shot past the Waxmans' all the way to the harbor and the little bait shop.

Pete looked in the other direction across Cyrus's pasture toward one of his favorite island sights—the bare winter branches of the apple trees on the hill. Pete supposed you couldn't really call this a working farm. Cyrus and Mary Pease got enough out of it to run a roadside vegetable stand in summer, to sell apples and cider in the fall, but there wasn't really any reason for Cyrus to be repairing fences in the bitter winter rain. There was, after all, no reason for them to come back each spring after their winter trip to Florida, yet come back they did. Why? Because this rock-filled farm was all the land they now owned?

Together, but not necessarily companionably, they set off across the field and eventually reached the barn. Cyrus swung open the heavy door and returned his tools to their proper pegs. Displayed against one wall of the barn was a well-kept-looking shotgun.

"Do you hunt, Cyrus?"

Cyrus shook his head. "Only woodchucks. And only if they're eating my tomatoes."

They walked as far as the house together. There was a Christmas wreath on Cyrus's door and Cyrus paused to straighten it.

Christmas.

Connie.

Why was it that this year every time Pete thought of Christmas he thought of Connie? It must, Pete thought, have something to do with the very nature of Christmas itself. The hope. The peace. The panic.

That night Pete's sister Polly called from Maine. Polly was two years younger than Pete, and there had been a day when those two years had catapulted Pete into the role of auxiliary parent, calling upon him to chauffeur where their parents wouldn't, understand what their parents didn't, solve what their parents couldn't. After a while Pete got demoted into plain old pal, but an emergency call straight from the old school still occasionally filtered through.

"They want me to go to Florida!" Polly wailed into the phone.

Pete pulled out a chair, always a key move when talking to Polly. "You don't have to," he said. "You can come here, like you usually do. The folks have things going on—they won't mind. It was their decision not to come up."

Silence.

"Hey?"

"Actually," said Polly, "I was thinking of staying up here."

"Oh." Pete suddenly pictured one lonely, limp Christmas stocking strung up on his fireplace. He closed his eyes.

"I've met this guy, Matthew . . ." And there followed a long description of Matthew. This entertaining Matthew. This intelligent Matthew. This *thoughtful* Matthew. This a-few-other-things-you'd-best-only-hint-to-your-brother-about Matthew.

"Oh," said Pete.

"But what should I tell Mom and Dad?"

"The truth," said Pete, an answer whose succinctness fell far short of their usual half-hour rehash of a reasonable white lie, and Polly seemed to catch the nuance.

"Hey! Why don't you come up here? Really! I want you to meet Matthew. We could have Christmas here, just the three of us. It's—"

"I don't know," said Pete. Third thumbing had never been his idea of a great time. "There's a lot going on around here right now." And he filled Polly in on Newby's death, partly, he knew, just because he wanted to change the subject.

Polly was stunned. "I can't believe this. *Newby*. He was just up here, hunting. I mean I just *saw* Newby two weeks ago. I can't believe this."

"He was up there? Alone?"

"He and the Boudreaux boys, that usual trip they take. Never hit anything, just hang out and play cards and drink beer and go play in the woods with their guns. They always stop by on the way up, since we're right off Route 1. Ozzie was just up here too, Newby said, a week or two before that, but Ozzie never stops. You know Ozzie. Hey, Pete, think about it, will you? It actually snows here. I mean, aren't you sick to death of spending Christmas in the *rain?*"

Pete didn't answer her. He was thinking about Newby and Ozzie hunting in Maine. Big game? Large-caliber rifles? Rifles that would be hanging in the bait shop right now?

But soon Polly was back on the subject of her new boyfriend, Matthew, repeatedly assuring Pete he would love him. Pete was sure he wouldn't. Polly had rotten taste in men.

"Well, think about Christmas, will you?"

"Sure," said Pete.

"And say hi to Connie if you see her." Polly always said that.

"Sure," said Pete.

The silence on the other end of the phone was a clear reminder that Pete didn't always say *that*.

Chapter
6

Rita Peck was starting to feel like she was the only person on earth who had ever heard of something called the Christmas spirit. True, Newby's funeral hadn't helped, and she had just gotten off the phone with her daughter, who was insisting that, despite the alternate-year rule worked out via the courts, she was going to spend her second year in a row with her father and his girlfriend. This made for a small difficulty, since Rita happened to know that Maxine's father and his girlfriend were planning to go to Belize, alone. Rita, always one to apply the charitable Christmas spirit the whole year round, had opted for the alternate-year rule argument instead of telling Maxine that she was not invited to Belize, and for her pains had just been rewarded with five minutes of screaming over the phone. Not to be daunted, she had gone out and purchased three packages of angel hair with which to decorate the Factotum office only to be met by a scowling Pete as he came through the door.

"I hate that stuff," he said. "Where are those green vines we've had every other year?"

"Beston's didn't *have* any green vines this year," said Rita. "If you don't like this, take it back and pick out something else."

"I like those green vines. Those green vines *go* in here." He waved at the plain pine walls and the lumpy rattan furniture.

"Fine," said Rita, her favorite word when things were least fine. "If you think I've got time to go traipsing all over the Hook looking for green *vines*, think again. I barely have time to buy Maxine's presents, although for all the aggravation that child is putting me through I've half a mind not to bother!" Rita sighed her weightiest sigh, and as he usually did when he heard it, Pete sat down on the corner of her desk to hear her out.

Rita poured out her day's dose of Maxine troubles.

"Christmas is tough on some," said Pete. "But you know Max—she'll come around in time."

Rita sighed. Yes, she would, and count on Pete to remind her of it. Of course Rita was well aware that Pete spent equally as much time coaching *Maxine* in her handling of her mother. It was a wonder that Pete continued to survive this job as father-on-call, and yes, Rita could admit it, a general all-around buffer of love between them.

Rita looked up at him with affection. "Now don't forget to be at the store at seven."

Pete looked blank.

"The carol sing. You told Evelyn you'd be there. *I* told Evelyn you'd be there. She's really counting on this to mend some of the rifts about the condos. And while we're on the subject of Christmas, you haven't done a single thing about your parents' room. There are twenty years of old newspapers piled up in there and about a—"

"They're not coming."

Rita looked at Pete in surprise. "Polly?"

He shook his head. "She's staying in Maine."

Rita looked at Pete hard, and for the first time she noticed that the past year had left some new creases in his outdoorsman's tan, especially around the eyes. Yes, Christmas *was* tough on some. *Darn* those people! Didn't they know how hard last Christmas was for Pete? And darn that Connie!

"You want to come with Maxine and me to Aunt Ethel's?"

Pete shook his head, but he smiled when he did it, and Rita felt a little perkier on his behalf. "So! The store at seven?"

Pete stopped smiling.

Now what was he so worried about, wondered Rita, Connie showing up? *Darn* that woman—why didn't she just stay away and leave him alone?

Pete had been unable to get the thought of Ozzie Dillingham's Maine hunting trip out of his mind. He had also begun to dwell on the question of whether Ozzie had really been at home the night of Sarah's party. It was no wonder that shortly after he left Factotum he found himself down at the harbor looking up at the peeling sign above the bait shop: DILLINGHAM BAIT AND TACKLE. BOATS TO RENT. CHARTER FISHING. CRAWLERS, SEA WORMS, SQUID, SAND EELS, SHINERS. Pete pushed open the door and was hit by the stench of a few of those choice items listed on the sign. He ducked under the low doorframe and followed his nose to the back.

Ozzie Dillingham was sitting on a stool at the back of the store, biting off a piece of fish line with his teeth. He looked a whole lot like Newby, with a similar full head of closely mown steel-gray hair and a round, weatherbeaten face beneath it, but Ozzie's eye was missing a certain twinkle that had always been present in Newby's. Ozzie's eye had something else in it—something that usually made people glad when he put out to sea.

"You're minding the store for a while?"

Ozzie looked behind him. "Don't see any volunteers."

"No."

"State your business."

Since Pete's business was none of his business, he paused for a minute to think. In typical Nashtoba fashion, Ozzie left him thinking and got up to go about his work. Pete nabbed him on the way by. "I'm real sorry about Newby."

"Why, you shoot him?"

"No, but I'd like to know who did. I suppose you would too. Polly says he stopped by on his way up north to hunt. What did he hunt—bear, moose, deer?"

"Why don't you ask him?"

Yes, Ozzie was a real beaut.

Pete picked a fishing lure off the rack next to him and idly read its wrapper. KETCH 'N' FETCH. NEW POWER CAST SURFACE LURE.

Ozzie disappeared, and returned with a tray of sand eels. The smell prompted Pete to try again. Fast.

"You hunt too?"

"Yup."

"A thirty-caliber bullet killed Newby. It isn't legal for hunting around here. I guess it must be somewhat rare?"

Ozzie snorted. He unbent himself from the stool and disappeared again. When he reappeared he had a rifle in each hand and a very Ozzie-like glint in his eye. Pete backed up.

"Know what this is?" Ozzie hefted one gun.

"No."

"Browning BAR. Know what this is?" He hefted the other.

"No."

56

"Remington 742."

There was a point here, and Pete figured he'd hurry Ozzie along toward it. "And?"

"Thirty-aught-six."

"Meaning?"

"Thirty meaning caliber, 1906, the year. Just about every manufacturer of bolt-action sporting rifles chambers the thirty-aught-six."

"So you're trying to tell me there are a few thirty-caliber rifles around. So what do you shoot with them?"

"Other than my brother, you mean?"

Pete got that point loud and clear. But surely Ozzie must realize he was in a somewhat precarious position, motivewise? And now here he was pointing the right type of rifle in Pete's face. Two of them. What was he, dumb? Pete decided it might be prudent to explain a few facts to Ozzie.

"You weren't at Sarah's party."

"Nope. Hear I missed out on a swell time."

"Yeah, swell." Pete was rapidly getting sick of Ozzie. He turned away, heading for the door.

"Don't know what came over me. Not like me to miss out on my brother being shot."

Pete reached the door and opened it.

Ozzie hollered after him. "And I missed out on hearing a roomful of people yammer at me about selling my shop! You think I want to be reeling in umbrella rigs the rest of my life? You think I couldn't use a half million dollars as much as the next fellow?"

"So now you can have it." Pete looked down at the rifles still dangling from Ozzie's fists. Ozzie raised both muzzles in the air. Pete scrunched his neck and closed his eyes, but there was no explosion, no feel of hot lead piercing his belly. He wasn't shot.

Pete knew the old adage: A gun was as safe as the person who used it. Figuring out who the unsafe people

57

were *before* they blew your head off—that was the problem.

When Pete returned to Factotum, Rita was at lunch and Allison Cox was staffing the desk.

Sort of. When Pete walked in she lifted her head from her crossed arms and stared at him with huge, tear-filled gray eyes, and Pete was all of a sudden reminded of her father and the ugly scene at the bank.

"Hey," said Pete.

Her head went back down. "Hey, Allison." Pete's vocabulary always seemed to desert him at times like these, especially around the monosyllabic Allison. He sat down on the corner of the desk and let one hand hover over her without coming to light. Her shoulder blades, as thin as bird's wings, protruded through her turtleneck shirt. "What's the matter?"

Silence. She burrowed deeper into her arms.

Pete heaved a great sigh, slid off the desk, and knelt down in front of Allison. "What's wrong?"

"They took his gun."

"Whose?"

"My father's."

"Your father's gun?"

"My grandfather's, really."

"Who, Willy? The chief?"

Allison's anguish finally unleashed her tongue. "And they wanted to know where he was that night Newby Dillingham got shot. He didn't know I was listening but I was, and I ran in and told them he was home with me." She looked straight at Pete now, her eyes still large and remarkably clear despite her recent tears, and Pete had a little trouble looking away from them.

"Mrs. Abrew didn't *invite* him to the party. Everybody's so mad at him because of the condos, and now the police are blaming him for *this*."

Pete, who pretty much organized Sarah's Christmas party for her these days, felt a twinge of guilt. "I'm sure they're just checking his gun as a matter of routine, but I could stop by the station and find out."

Allsion raised her eyes, those transfixing gray eyes. "Thank you."

"Sure," said Pete. "I'll go right now." But for some reason he was still riveted to the spot, eyes locked with Allison's, when Rita came through the door laden with Christmas packages.

The police station was buzzing. Willy's voice could be heard talking into the phone all the way down the hall. Paul Roose raced from one room to another, Ted Ball typed madly, Jean Martell whispered into the head-set and darted looks over her shoulder to see who was listening, her face a picture of torment as she spied Pete. What to do, what to do? Continue to pass on news over the wires or hang up fast and bleed Pete for what she could?

Pete nabbed Paul as he raced by. "You've brought in a gun of Nate Cox's?"

Paul nodded. "Nineteen-oh-three Springfield."

Pete nodded as if this might mean something to him, but Paul wasn't fooled.

"One of the older bolt-action rifles from World War One, but they used them after Pearl Harbor when so many men enlisted that they ran out of M-1's. Terrible gun. Complicated sight, nearly kicked your shoulder off."

Jean Martell crept up behind them. "Nate's had been recently fired. It's thirty caliber. We haven't heard from the lab on the bullet—the chief only just sent the gun down." She cocked an ear. "I think that's them on the phone right now. About the bullet, I'd guess."

Pete turned to Paul. "But does Nate's gun really matter? Nate Cox was with his daughter that night."

Paul raised an eyebrow. "Yeah? I hear she does a lot for her father."

Pete had heard so too—from Rita once and from Andy twice. "Willy doesn't believe her?"

"I wouldn't know." Paul moved away.

"Hey, wait a minute!"

"Can't. Errand to run." He gave a cynical push to the word *errand*.

Somehow Pete managed to scoot past Jean and make his way down the hall to Willy's office. He arrived as Willy was just hanging up the phone.

"Well?" said Pete.

Willy stared down at the notebook in front of him, its long yellow surface marked with dark black script. "Preliminary lab report on the bullet. Thirty-aught-six. Military."

"Nate's Springfield. Paul said that was military. Was it—"

Like a returning ghost, Paul Roose spoke from the doorway. "Thirty-aught-six. But the fact that it's a military round doesn't mean it's being used in a military rifle. Government ammunition's plenty available. And cheap."

Willy squinted at Paul. Willy's squint started below the eyes and ended at his hairline, giving it a long way to go these days.

"So how much has this narrowed things down?" asked Pete.

"Not much. If we had the cartridge case, we'd have better luck."

Isn't that always the way, thought Pete. You give them the bullet, they want the case. "So where's the case apt to be?"

"Probably within five or six yards of where the killer

stood," said Paul. "We were hoping he'd have been in enough of a rush, it being at night and all, that he wouldn't bother to retrieve it when he left."

Paul handed a folded half sheet to the chief. "Here's a list of the Gun Club's members." He turned to Pete. "This sniper can shoot," he explained. "We thought it might be helpful to know who's keeping his hand in."

"So you still haven't narrowed down the weapon? It could be the Springfield, or a Browning BAR, or a Remington 742?"

The two policemen looked up at Pete, in accord for once.

"Who's got a Browning BAR or a Remington 742?"

After only the smallest of hesitations, Pete told Willy about the rifles in Dillingham's bait shop.

"Not much of a gun place, huh?" Willy headed out the door, presumably for Dillingham Bait and Tackle.

Pete headed for the door after him, but not before he leaned over to peek at Paul's list. Most of the names on the list were familiar to Pete—surprisingly so. When *had* Nashtoba become so gun crazy? But some of the names were of particular interest, among them *both* of the Dillingham brothers, as well as Cyrus Pease.

Chapter

7

Connie Bartholomew was not by nature a moody person. Somewhat quick-tempered, maybe, apt to be a bit brusque, perhaps, but moody—no. She was also not a very solitary person, and after her return to Nashtoba she frequently found her two rooms over Coolidge's garage either growing in on her or expanding out, becoming alternately too small or two big. Connie wasn't used to living alone. She wasn't used to thinking of Christmas as one long and lonely ride to New Jersey and back.

Connie liked Christmas. She wasn't one of those people who suffered through the whole Christmas season just because of a little thing like her whole life falling apart. Connie looked at Christmas as a sort of life raft. Here it was the darkest, gloomiest, dreariest time of the year, when loneliness couldn't possibly get much lonelier, and just when it seems there is absolutely nothing to do and no one to do it with, along comes Christmas. Lights spring up in the darkness. Songs cut through the dead air. There's stuff to do. Christmas shopping, Christmas decorating, Christmas cards, Christmas *movies*. Connie jumped off the couch to look at the calendar. How many days till Christmas? Thirteen. She supposed that to many people thirteen days was not enough, but to Connie, whose shopping methods could best be described as short and to the point, all of a sudden it seemed that she had an awful lot of days left to go and not enough Christmasy things to do in them.

Connie looked at the calendar again. Wait a minute—tonight was the night of Evelyn Waxman's carol sing at Beston's Store. It was just like Evelyn Waxman, one of those causy women of boundless energy, to organize everything she got her hands on—even Christmas. But a carol sing? It was pretty corny, thought Connie, but then again, she'd always had this motto: if it's broke, fix it. If the room's too small, too big, too lonely—get the hell out of there. Fast.

Connie threw on her coat and headed for Beston's Store.

The closer she got to the store, the worse the idea seemed. Lanterns bobbed and blazed from the porch roof of Beston's Store, and Connie could pick out the faces in the crowd: Rita Peck and Evan Spender, Maxine and her boyfriend Todd, Jerry and Betsy Beggs, and Andy Oatley with the Beggs's daughter Jill. Everywhere else she looked the people seemed to be in small family groups or pairs. Even Evelyn Waxman, illuminated by one of the lanterns above her head as she stood on the steps of the store, could look to the edge of the crowd and see her husband, Jim, and their three kids. But wait a minute—who was that lone soul lurking so far in the rear, facing the wrong way, mouth not moving with song?

Pete.

Should she go talk to him? Connie felt uncharacteristically indecisive. Maybe he was alone because he wanted to be alone. He had always been a person at home with himself, able to entertain himself without the help of outside stimuli. Maybe being alone was only a crime to those who were uncomfortable with their own thoughts. And besides, what made Connie think Pete would be at all interested in *her* company? One silly episode of empathy over her strange fatigue at Sarah's, one act of kindness in the form of a short ride home? Maybe he was at the far end of the crowd with his back to her because he had seen her coming. That was most likely the truth of the matter, if recent history was any judge. Connie about-faced and moved in the opposite direction as far and as fast as she could go, so that she was standing in clear sight of Evelyn Waxman when the lantern above Evelyn's head exploded and glass rained around her onto the ground.

Several people shrieked, but since Evelyn Waxman continued to stand on the steps among the litter of glass grinning out at the crowd as if any minute now she would burst into song, nobody but Connie moved to help her. Evelyn's forehead had already turned dark from the blood running out of her head by the time Connie reached her side.

"You're bleeding," said Connie. "Why don't you sit down?"

"Don't be silly," said Evelyn. "Why would I be bleeding?"

Connie jammed Evelyn down onto the store steps and pawed through her stiff salt-and-pepper hair. "Possibly because your head's full of glass."

"Glass? *Glass*. What *glass*. This glass?" Evelyn tried to stand up and kicked a crepe-soled shoe across some pieces of glass on the steps. "In my *head?* Oh, for heaven's sake. Glass."

Connie encouraged Evelyn to stay sitting by a hand

jammed downward on her shoulder. Connie looked
around, spying George Beston. "George. She's pretty
cut up. Call the rescue, will you?" George Beston ran
inside to use the phone. Jerry Beggs pushed forward
and handed Connie a handkerchief, something Connie
hadn't seen in years. She started to mop up Evelyn's
face, which grew whiter in direct proportion to how dark
the handkerchief became.

"That's me," said Evelyn, staring at the handkerchief. "Bleeding."

"Not much," Connie lied.

Jim Waxman finally reached Evelyn's side, having sta-
tioned his children with a bystander, and the look on
his face did more to alarm Evelyn than the sight of her
own blood had. "I'm *bleeding,* Jim." She wavered on
the steps.

"Get a blanket or something," Connie said to Jim.

"Get a blanket or something!" Jim yelled into the
crowd. Those who had tightened in around the steps
parted. First a blanket arrived, then Ernie Ball, the vol-
unteer fireman, arrived, then his son, policeman Ted
Ball, and finally, thankfully, Connie saw the police
chief's head and shoulders plowing toward the steps.
She backed out of the way, noting with some surprise
that her hands were shaking now that she no longer
needed them to be still. She wandered away from the
steps, looking through the disintegrating edges of the
crowd for Pete, but she couldn't see him. She moved
into the thick of the crowd and looked again, but Pete
was nowhere in sight. Suddenly she heard what people
were saying.

"Shot! It was a shot! Another shot! Someone shot
Evelyn!"

"Evelyn's shot! Evelyn's shot!" The cry moved
around Connie. Pete was nowhere. Something seemed
to suck at her breath. She pushed away from the congeal-

ing mob to look for Pete, straining against the dark, concentrating on the ground, calling his name.

Evelyn Waxman swung into the crowd on a stretcher, and if the state of her organizational skills was anything to go by, she appeared to be doing all right.

"They're taking me to the doctor's. No, Jim, I'm perfectly all right. Perfectly all right. Take the children home and stay with them—I'll call you there. No, the chief's coming after me to ask me some questions—he's going to get me home. Make sure Althea picks up the sheet music. And remind her to check the restroom and lock the door. The sheet music, Jim. And put out the fire in the oil drum!"

Evelyn sailed off, and Connie went after the chief, who was digging something out of the front of Beston's Store. Connie grabbed his arm. "Pete's gone. He was standing in the back. The shots—"

The chief stopped digging. "What do you mean, shots? More than one?"

"I don't know," Connie admitted. "But even if it was just one! One bullet went through Sarah's window and Newby's head and my jacket. One bullet supposedly went through the governor of Texas and the President of the United States! Pete's not—"

"Pete's not what?" said Pete from behind them, and Connie jumped.

"Got it," said the chief. He stopped digging in the wall and held up something Connie was dismayed to find she could now recognize as a bullet.

"And I got *this*," said Pete, and he held up a tubular coppery thing. He looked at the chief first, and then he looked at Connie. "Are you all right?"

"*Me*," said Connie. "Me? Of course I'm all right."

"Evelyn. Is she—"

"Evelyn's all right," said Willy. "Now show me where you found that."

The police chief moved away. Pete looked at Connie again. "Are you sure you're—"

"Oh, for God's sake," said Connie, "I'm all right."

Pete followed Willy, looking behind him as he did so. Connie sat down on the steps. Her knees were shaking as well.

Chapter
8

Pete leaned against Hardy Rogers's examining room wall as the doctor picked splinters of glass out of Evelyn Waxman's head. The chief, delayed on the hill where Pete had taken him, had assigned this job to Pete—to follow Evelyn, to make sure she was all right, to drive her home once the doctor was through, and apparently, to answer Evelyn's questions.

"It was a *bullet*, Pete? Do you mean to say a bullet? Do you mean they actually found a bullet?"

"Stop twisting your head, Evelyn, goddammit." After nine o'clock at night Hardy left his bedside manner back at home beside his own bed, along with his lab coat. He yanked up the sleeves of a moth-eaten old sweater and dove back into Evelyn's scalp.

"Willy found the bullet, I found the casing," Pete answered Evelyn. Pete was kind of proud of that part. True, it was a stroke of luck that he had been facing backward just when the gun muzzle had flashed on the hill. Well, no, actually, it was a stroke of cowardice. He'd seen her, seen Connie, drawing closer and closer to the store, and had been afraid to see which way she'd go. Toward him? Away from him? He had turned away, facing the dark hill behind Cox's realty office, and had seen the flash. It was amazing, really, how fast he had connected it all—the flash, the exploding lantern, Evelyn Waxman's bloody head. There had seemed to be plenty of people close to Evelyn to help out there, so Pete had grabbed his flashlight from the truck and had shot across the street without thinking any further. He had charged toward the flash of light, pacing out his hundred yards, thinking about what he had learned at Sarah's about trajectory, not thinking much about things he probably should have been thinking about, like getting shot himself. There had been only one clear spot, one visible patch of ground in the vicinity of the flash, and it hadn't taken Pete long to find the copper metal tube on the ground, the very cartridge casing the chief had looked for at Newby's shooting and had been unable to find. What had Paul Roose said? The sniper had probably stood within five or six yards of the spot where Pete found the casing. Pete had snapped off a small dead branch and jammed it into the ground to mark the spot for Willy, the very spot Willy was still combing right now.

Evelyn Waxman winced as Hardy jabbed at her scalp again. "You can't seriously be finding *more* glass. Not *more* glass?"

"Hold still. Christ on a raft! If you'd stay home once in a while, Evelyn, you wouldn't have a head full of glass. You're lucky it's not a head full of lead. You're lucky he's losing his aim."

Evelyn's head whirled around to look at Pete just as Hardy began to probe again and, consequently, missed. "You can't mean . . . you can't seriously be thinking . . . you don't mean to say that he was *aiming* at me?"

Pete looked at Hardy Rogers. The steel-blue eyes looked at Pete and back down at the bloody battlefield.

Pete cleared his throat. "I suppose once the chief gets to compare the two bullets we'll know more about whether this is the same sniper or not. As to whether he was aiming at you—"

"Well, he wasn't," said Evelyn with a decisive nod that caused Hardy to slam his tweezers, sans glass, into the metal tray.

"Let me know when you're through dancing all over the office, will you, Evelyn?"

"Well, he wasn't aiming at me. He simply wasn't. No one in their right mind would try to *shoot* me. Not *shoot* me."

Pete had to wonder. Pete had done a few jobs for Evelyn Waxman, one of which had kept him lying on his belly for twelve hours at a stretch counting assorted water fowl, another of which had him replanting and bolstering up trampled beach grass, both jobs in the very sand dune Ozzie's condominiums would erase. Evelyn was intense about the sand dunes. Evelyn was also intense about her petition for the moratorium on waterfront development. Evelyn's was the kind of intense that usually got things done, and that kind of intense could be pretty threatening. To some.

"I don't know, Evelyn. That conservation group you're in charge of must be putting a good scare into CRAP."

"Oh, *CRAP*," said Hardy.

Evelyn Waxman drew herself up higher. Hardy grabbed her by the ear and held tight.

"Ow! Doctor Rogers! Ow. You're . . . Oh, dear. All right. Really, Pete. My petition is no cause for me to be *shot*. Not shot. I mean . . . shot?"

She looked at Pete, without moving her head this time, her face finally paling in the glare of Hardy's overhead light.

"Shot?" she asked one more time, as the final splinter of glass tinkled into the metal tray.

* * *

Pete leaned over his beer at Lupo's and listened to the police chief describe his investigation of the spot on the hill Pete had marked for him. He had found no further clues, but he was clearly pleased to have the casing, and something of Pete's own self-satisfaction must have glimmered—across the booth the police chief grinned.

"All right, all right, first a bullet, then a cartridge casing. I'll give you a list of what else I need. Although it was a stupid thing to do, you know that? Your wife was running around out of her mind, thinking you'd been shot."

Pete's head shot up out of his beer. "Who, Connie?"

"Oh, yeah, sorry. Ex-wife. I keep forgetting." Still, the chief grinned.

A thickened figure in a navy blue suit with a fringe of graying sandy hair pushed itself off a stool at the bar and sauntered over.

"Pete."

"Nate."

"*Chief.*" There the realtor's voice changed, not for the better. "When do I get my gun back, huh? I'd like to know since when is it a crime to make money around here."

"You're making some money?" asked Willy politely.

Nate Cox's eyes, already considerably camouflaged by fat, seemed to disappear further, and Pete wondered how the birdlike Allison was going to look at his age. "I will be. I'll be making plenty. Soon."

"Were you in the service, Mr. Cox?" Willy asked.

The realtor rested his palms on the edge of the booth and then rested his weight on his palms. "Was I in the service? I was in a war. A *real* war. You probably think you fought in one but it was nothing, nothing, I tell you, compared to what we accomplished, what we went

71

through. Or maybe you didn't fight in one at all. Maybe you were one of those dodge-to-Canada types.''

Pete looked nervously at the bar, where to his knowledge at least two Vietnam vets, Abel Cobb and Wally Melville, were twisting around, suddenly looking a little restless in their seats.

"Hardship deferment," said Willy. He seemed in no rush to untangle himself from Nate's whiskey-sodden ramblings about the guts and glory of the Good War, but finally he pushed himself out of the booth, dwarfing the heavy realtor but somehow managing to look sorry as he did so. He wasn't a man who threw his weight around much.

Pete followed him out of the bar. "What was that all about?"

"We got a further report from the lab on that first bullet you found. Not only was the bullet military, but it was fired from a military barrel. Nate Cox's Springfield is a military rifle. The lab hasn't run through the ballistics tests on it yet, but I thought I might as well ask a few questions early on."

So take that, Bert! thought Pete, but amid all the cold, hard scientific facts he suddenly remembered the crumbling face of Allison, and all his enthusiasm drained away. "Allison says it was her grandfather's rifle. Paul Roose corroborates that—he says Nate's rifle was from the First World War."

"So what if it is? It still works, doesn't it? It takes the same ammunition. And what about Nate Cox's weapon from the *Second* World War? Not that you're supposed to walk out of a war with your weapons. Misappropriation of government property. But a lot of fellows got pretty sentimental about their guns. If his father stole one, maybe Nate stole another to complete the set. It was easy enough to do. But we're starting with the one we were able to find. So exactly how worked up *is*

Evelyn Waxman over the Connor, Rice and Peterson project?"

Pete told the chief a little of how Evelyn felt about sand dunes and about the assorted grasses, plants, and water fowl that lived there.

"But her moratorium on waterfront development is aimed directly at this planned CRAP project, am I correct?"

Pete nodded.

Willy looked almost as pleased with this news as he had over the cartridge case.

"You think someone was really trying to shoot Evelyn?"

"I think I'm going to Boston to see this Connor, Rice and Peterson."

"CRAP?"

"Crap," said Willy, with an awful lot of feeling for a relative newcomer, Pete thought.

When Pete got home the phone was already ringing. He banged through the door, snatching up the phone. *She was running around out of her mind, thinking you'd been shot?* "Hello!" he hollered into the phone, trying to make up with volume what he had lacked in speed.

"Don't shout, dear. I may be old but my hearing is still excellent."

"Hi, Mom." Pete's enthusiasm, as well as his voice, dropped down a few registers.

"Hello, dear. Now who's this Matthew your sister's suddenly talking so much about?"

Pete sat down on Rita's desk. In many ways Pete's sister Polly was nothing like himself—when Pete announced he was planning to marry Connie his parents had justifiably asked, *"Who?"* With Polly, on the other hand, details and descriptions flowed back and forth over the phone wires ad infinitum. Ad nauseam! The fact that she never married any of them used to greatly annoy their mother until Pete got divorced. Now all Polly heard, or so she told Pete, was "Take your time, dear. Think it over. No sense rushing into things."

"I don't know, some guy."

"Well, you'll find out at Christmas. She says you're going to Maine? That will be very nice."

Pete looked at the phone, suddenly and completely out of sorts. "Nobody said I was going to Maine."

"Oh! Then you'll come down here! Ralph, he's coming down here!"

"Nobody said I was doing that, either!"

"Well, dear, if you *do* plan on coming down, I think you'd better get your ticket. There are only thirteen more days till Christmas, you know."

"I *know* how many days there are till Christmas."

His mother paused, indicating disapproval of his tone. "So. Polly told me about poor Newby. I might say you could have mentioned it yourself, you know. Have they caught the fellow yet?"

"No," said Pete. "And now he's taken a shot at Evelyn Waxman." Only as Pete said it did he realize he must have taken Willy's pending visit to CRAP as the answer to the question of whether someone had purposely shot at Evelyn.

"My lord! Killed her? Is she . . ."

"She's all right. She was standing on the steps of Beston's Store under this glass lantern that exploded when the bullet hit."

"My lord. I don't think it sounds very safe up there. Why don't you leave right now, take a little holiday, come see us down here?"

Sometimes with his mother less was better than more. "I can't," said Pete, and with only one final, prolonged sigh, his mother hung up the phone.

He didn't want to go to Florida. But he didn't want to go to Maine. Christmas was supposed to be here on

Nashtoba. Christmas was supposed to be a fire in his own fireplace, popcorn in his favorite red and white bowl, Connie's feet up on the end of the couch and her head in his lap.

She was running around out of her mind.

So who said Pete had to go to Florida or Maine? Who said he couldn't stay here by himself? Or maybe *not* by himself?

Christmas. Connie. Suddenly the whole equation seemed to tip a little more toward hope and a little less toward panic. There *had* been minutes of late, minutes that had been almost all right—a shared thought by Sarah's bedside, a look exchanged while finding the bullet in the coat—and hadn't there been a little something later that same night riding home in Pete's truck? And at Evelyn Waxman's shooting she had been running around out of her mind, thinking he'd been shot. So what did it all mean—other than that they seemed to thrive best in violent surroundings? Couldn't Pete do something, say something to break this impasse? But what? Pete spent most of the night wracking his brain for just the right excuse that would carry him into Connie's presence once more, short of having to kill someone himself.

He hadn't thought of a thing by the time Willy McOwat phoned the next morning with more news.

The cartridge case indeed confirmed that it was military ammunition, but it also contained a particular type of corrosive primer that had, for all practical purposes, been obsolete since the Second World War.

"What!"

"The ammunition is old, Pete. It may not mean much if it's military, but it sure as hell means a few things if it's old."

"Why?"

"Who uses it? You can't even count on the stuff to

75

work! Now I'm off to Boston and CRAP. But think about it, will you? Old ammunition, Pete. Who'd use it?''

Pete thought about it all right and got nothing except more curious. He hung around long enough to see how Allison was bearing up, but was unable to decipher the gaze in the gray eyes or to get much out of her in the way of speech. He concluded that for Allison this was pretty normal.

He went next to Sarah's, where the Mormon Tabernacle Choir singing "Deck the Halls" told him all he needed to know about *her* spirits. It didn't do anything to harm his, either. He left Sarah's for the Gun Club whistling.

The Nashtoba Gun Club looked just about exactly as Pete had expected. The structure itself was a real log cabin, with a long function room with a massive fireplace at the far end flanked by stuffed heads of things that were rumored to be full of fleas. Stretching beyond the cabin itself was the rifle range, and behind that, woods that Pete could only hope were nice and thick.

He walked into the lodge and found Bob Chase, member-in-charge, swabbing down a Formica countertop in a surprisingly modern kitchen. Bob looked just about exactly like a member-in-charge should, Pete thought: flannel shirt, heavy twill trousers, suspenders, duck boots. He began by asking Bob if anyone ever used old ammunition that dated back to World War II and was surprised at his answer.

"We have a whole bunch of fellas who use that stuff every week. They shoot with nothing but the old military guns, and the old ammo to boot. Authenticity, see?''

"No," said Pete, who didn't.

"It's a military shoot. They come in Sundays and compete using the old weapons and the old ammo. You're using an M-1 Garand, a carbine, an old Springfield, you don't want to use new ammo—it's not legit. Trying to recreate the exact conditions, see?''

Finally Pete saw. ''And who participates in these military shoots? Do you have a list?''

''A list? I suppose I could rustle up the last shoot's roster.'' Bob Chase narrowed his eyes a little at Pete. ''Any particular reason?''

''Police business,'' said Pete, amazed that the stupid answer worked, especially since the police didn't seem to be too popular with Bob.

''Police business! You'd think they could do their own legwork, wouldn't you? Free club memberships from the town, rifle range reserved special for their training . . .'' He drifted off and returned with a raggedly torn off piece of paper. Most of the names on this list were unfamiliar to Pete, probably off-islanders drawn to Nashtoba for this specialized shoot, but among the names there was one he knew: Cyrus Pease.

''About this old ammunition,'' Pete continued. ''Would anyone ever use it in a new gun?''

Bob Chase scratched his jaw. ''New gun. Can't see why. Not reliable. Why bother? Unless you found an old box of it lying around in the attic somewhere and wanted to use it up. There's plenty of newer surplus military ammo to be had cheap.''

So Willy would be looking for an old military rifle from World War II or earlier. Was anyone from the island still alive who had fought in World War I? Pete didn't think so. That meant looking for World War II vets. That meant back to Nate Cox. Pete thought again of Allison. ''This M-1 something that you mentioned . . .''

''Garand. That was the standard rifle in the Second World War. Issued about five million of them. The carbine was lighter, came along later—that was used in the South Pacific a lot.''

"What caliber guns are all these?"

"Thirty," said Bob, not much to Pete's surprise. "The Garand uses a thirty-aught-six, the carbine a straight pistol-type thirty-caliber cartridge, not interchangeable with the other. Now let me tell you something about the carbine . . ."

It was many minutes and a lot more guns later before Pete bumped down the rutted road away from the Gun Club trying to remember just how many days ago he had told the chief Nashtoba wasn't much of a gun place. *Hah!*

"CRAP!" Bert Barker shouted once Pete crossed the floorboards toward the stove at Beston's Store. "Some shell-shocked Nazi hater's running around sniping at us and that lousy cop's in Boston trying to find CRAP! I want that cop on twenty-four-hour alert right here on this island, that's what I want! I want him where we can see him, where we know what he's doing to earn that salary I'm busting my butt to pay!" Bert leaned back against the wood bench where his butt had just about worn a hole by now and sipped his coffee.

"What do you say, Pete?" asked Ed Healey. "An old military bullet. Poor Newby! And poor Evelyn. That bullet wasn't two feet over her head."

"Poor Evelyn? Serve her right for sticking her nose in where it doesn't belong!"

"It was a damned close shot," said Evan.

"Must have been Nate Cox," said Bert, and for some reason that set Ed's many chins vibrating with humor.

But certainly the evidence against Nate seemed to be mounting fast. He owned the right kind of old military weapon. He was out on a terrible financial limb and could only climb back to safety through sale of the condominium development. He had been absent from both sniper scenes. As if that weren't enough, now Bert Barker was adding even more to his plate.

"After all, Nate's the big expert marksman, right, Ed?"

Ed nodded. "Expert. Says so right on his discharge papers. He'll show you anytime you ask."

"Yep," continued Bert. "Deadeye Cox." For some reason that set Ed off for good. He threw back his head and roared into the air, and even Evan Spender grinned.

Pete felt the sweat run straight down his spine. He didn't think any of this was funny. He should have expected the men around the stove to rally against any newcomer where they could, but all he could think of was Allison's eyes, and Newby, and Evelyn, and whoever it was that the sniper might take down next.

"Nate's not the only one under suspicion," said Pete.

"Hell, no," said Bert. "Old Ozzie'd shoot his brother for stepping on his toe."

"But would he shoot Evelyn, Bert?" asked Ed.

"If she waved that petition under his nose too close he would!"

"But does he have anything military lying around? I never saw it if he did." Ed shook his head. "Nate Cox and the Springfield. I'll lay ten dollars on it."

"There are plenty other military weapons lying around," said Evan. "What about Buck's M-1?"

"Buck Bacon?"

"Buck Bacon," said Bert. "He smuggled it home on the troop ship and has been cleaning it ever since. Better make sure Nate doesn't get his hands on it, right, Ed?"

Ed didn't answer. He was too busy wiping tears of mirth off his face.

Chapter
9

Pete's next job of the day was to help decorate the Whiteaker Hotel for Christmas. The old Victorian hotel sat right on Close Harbor, facing the dock, an upper-class neighbor of Dillingham Bait and Tackle. Jack Whiteaker had kept the old rambling hotel open through the few good economic times and the long spells of bad, bringing Pete to conclude that there was other money somewhere—a conclusion further supported by the fact that Jack often hired Factotum to do many minor jobs for him, Christmas decorating being only one. Pete and Connie used to choose to do this particular job themselves, starting at opposite ends of the long veranda and winding the bows of holly and red ribbon around each pillar, making the race to the middle a holiday tradition of their own. Last year Pete had unloaded the job onto the rest of Factotum's crew; this year he'd stalled until he'd been stuck doing it alone. What if he called Connie right now and asked her to help? Pete snorted. If he was going to call her he should just call her—he shouldn't have to use Whiteaker's pillars as a wedge! So why *didn't* he just call her? Pete had left off winding holly so as to argue with himself more efficiently when Jack Whiteaker pulled up in his van.

"Take a look at this, Pete." Jack held up a half-inch long hollow metal tube. "I found this in my driveway. Think the police should take a look at it?"

It was a cartridge casing, but much smaller than the one Pete had found on the hillside across from Beston's Store.

"I'm sure they should."

"And soon, too, I'd figure." Jack looked at his watch. "I can't leave now, I'm expecting someone. How does Factotum handle abrupt changes in job description? Could you run this over to the station, and I'll finish the holly instead?"

Factotum handled abrupt changes in job description much better than its owner handled abrupt changes in life, Pete thought. He cheerfully exchanged Christmas for crime and headed off for the station.

The only one around was Paul Roose. He took the cartridge casing from Pete, managing to look unimpressed.

"Nine millimeter. Nothing to do with your sniper." He put it in his pocket.

"Oh." Pete wondered if it was healthy to feel disappointed. He looked around. "Where is everyone?"

"Chief's still in Boston. Ted's on some wild-goose chase to some gun shop over on the Hook. Jean's on some three-hour lunch. I'm on the desk." Pete looked at Paul's snidely turned mouth and decided that this was not a happy camper. But why should he be? Strictly according to Hoyle, the much less senior Ted Ball should be minding store while Paul tracked down leads on the Hook, wild-goose chases or not. Obviously Paul had a lot of knowledge about guns. What could the twenty-three-year-old Ted Ball have that could compete with that? Wasn't the chief taking this thing a little too far?

"I hear a rumor that Nate Cox is an expert marksman. I don't recall seeing his name on the Gun Club's list."

Paul rummaged around behind the desk and extracted the list. He looked it over. "No."

"That's funny," said Pete, but since Paul didn't respond, he added, "Isn't it? Wouldn't an expert want to stay an expert? I gathered from you that to keep your hand in requires a certain amount of work."

Paul chewed the corner of his lip and let his face wrinkle and divide into the myriad geometric creases that salt spray and wind brought early to Nashtoba faces. "Suppose so." He rolled a form into an old manual typewriter and began to type.

"I suppose there are other rifle ranges?"

Paul began to list them without raising his head. "Public range in Bradford. Anyone can apply for a permit and get a key. Arapo Sportsman's Club. Huntsman's Lodge in Naushon. Rod and Gun Club at Weam's Point."

"Wow," said Pete in his best Hardy Boys voice.

Paul kept typing.

"Shouldn't someone run over there and check them out? See if Nate's listed?"

Paul shrugged. "I might if I ran the zoo. I might if I could get *out* of the zoo." He typed on.

"And have a talk with Buck Bacon." Pete was really wired now. He told Paul about Buck's M-1, and the typewriter keys stalled, but Paul shook his head.

"I only work here."

"So how about if *I* go?"

Paul looked at Pete. He said nothing, but his eyes glinted.

Going to the Hook was always fairly depressing for Pete. For one thing, it always seemed to preview for him what his more pristine island might someday become, and for another, every time he passed the Port-O-Call Motel in Arapo and saw the sign TWENTY DOLLARS FOR TWO! he kept picturing Glen and Connie inside.

Okay, grow up, Pete lectured himself this time. He left the motel behind him and pulled onto Main Street. "Jingle Bell Rock" blasted off-key through a tinny speaker somewhere, every street lamp had a twist of the hated angel hair running up its base, and shoppers were hopping in and out of stores in thick drizzle. Pete grinned. How could he leave all this for Florida, for Maine? Who said he had to, anyway? She'd been running around out of her mind, thinking he'd been shot. He'd call Connie. He would! He drove on to the Sportsman's Club picturing two fat stockings on his fireplace.

As an excuse to look at the club membership lists Pete had managed to concoct a plausible enough story about a gift membership for his uncle Nate Cox unless he had already joined, but he soon found that the Hook was so jaded they didn't even care why he wanted to know what he wanted to know. Nate Cox, however, was not a member of any of the clubs, and it was only at the public range that Pete struck anything resembling pay dirt. On December 8, the day after Newby's murder, Nate had signed onto the range. Pete flipped back through the book but couldn't find any other entries for Nate, which seemed surprising. He went to a range and practiced *once?* The day *after* the first shooting? Maybe he thought he needed the practice. But why, after a shot that dispatched Newby so cleanly?

Pete gave that more thought as he returned to the island. What if Nate Cox shot Newby and then ran to the range the next day to shoot again in case the police stumbled upon his gun and saw that it had been recently fired, as was indeed the case? Here was documented proof of where and when he had fired it. So why hadn't Nate told the cops about it then? Pete gave up.

He tracked Buck Bacon down at Knackie's, the fisherman's bar on the far side of the island. Buck was at the bar, still wrapped up in watch cap, down parka, and a red and green scarf. Other than Buck's scarf and the Rudolph-like redness to the noses of some of the patrons, no other Christmas decor was visible here.

Pete approached the bar. "Hey, Buck."

"Hey! Pete!"

Buck ordered beers for both of them. Pete paid for them. It helped.

Buck launched right in on the subject of the sniper. "Ain't that something, an old piece of ammunition like that?"

"Strange," agreed Pete. "That's why I wanted to talk to you. You were in the war?"

"I followed Patton's Third Army clear across all Europe! And you know what I remember most? The girls. I tell you. Maybe Patton got the glory, but I'm the one who got hugged!" Buck laughed, but judging by the meager responses from his fellow bar patrons to the left and right, Pete suspected the line had been worn thin by overuse.

Buck was off and running. Pete nursed his one beer, nodded at Buck as he listened, and thought about Nate Cox's prideful tales. What was it about the veterans of this older war? Where were the scars that Vietnam had left on his own generation? As Buck talked Pete's attention was caught by an old fisherman two stools down whose hands began to shake violently.

Buck saw him and whispered to Pete. "Anzio."

Was that it? Were there just as many walking wounded from the older wars who were hiding their pain, who had not yet learned it was healing to speak of the bad as well as the "good"?

Buck fell quiet, but by now Pete knew what he had come to find out. In a right-of-passage ceremony Buck had handed over his precious, stolen M-1 to his son Fred, who, Buck said, treasured it as if it had been his very own.

Pete left Knackie's in search of Fred, and in typical island fashion found him in the first place he looked, the market. Pete wasn't surprised—Fred had been working there for twenty years.

Pete remembered Fred from school as a fellow with little curiosity. He apparently hadn't picked up any since.

"Pop's old gun?" Fred repeated, no questions asked. "Yeah, he gave it to me. I sold it to Cyrus for seventy-five bucks."

"Cyrus?"

"Pease. You know. The collector. Said it was in mint condition. Probably stole it off me, but what do I know? Seventy-five bucks is seventy-five bucks."

Pete was beginning to think that the very island structure was resting precariously on trunks and boxes and barrels full of guns. He had not known that Cyrus was a collector. He drove straight from the supermarket to the farm.

The house was locked up. A huge padlock swung from the barn door. Gone. He got back in the truck and continued on his way, but as he passed the Waxmans' he spotted Evelyn's bright bandage as she walked across her yard with a cardboard box in her hands. She waved wildly. Pete pulled in.

"How's the head?"

"Oh, all right. All right. The head's all right. If you're looking for the Peases, they've left for Florida."

"I *was* looking for them. Do you happen to know where they're staying down there?"

Evelyn put the box down on a stump, and Pete was not surprised to see it was full of Christmas decorations. Evelyn Waxman was not the type to let a little thing like a head full of glass put a damper on her holiday spirits.

"I do happen to know that. I do. Though no thanks to Cyrus Pease, I can tell you that. What an old pill! I've got the address inside. Come on."

They went inside. The first thing Pete saw on the kitchen table was Evelyn's petition, and Evelyn followed his gaze.

"Yes, the police chief just brought it back. I don't know what he wanted with it. I think it's silly. I really think it's silly. I refuse to even think about it. I absolutely refuse."

Pete glanced down the long list of signatures and was surprised to see the names of both Cyrus and Mary Pease.

"Now here," said Evelyn. "Look at this. Here's the address and phone number of the condominium the Peases have rented in Florida, and it was like pulling teeth to get this out of them. What did they think we wanted it for, I ask you? 'Just in case something goes wrong at the farm,' I said, and Cyrus looked at me as if he thought I'd try to burn it down just so I could call him and tell him about it! We only suggested it at all because of that loft door blowing off the first year. Jim and I offered to keep an eye on the place for them the first winter we were here but Cyrus rebuffed us in no uncertain terms. He said some of his own would take care of it. After the door incident Jim asked for the address again and Cyrus said no, but later Mary came over and left it." Evelyn gazed distractedly at the piece of paper. "You know, now that I think about it, buying this place from the Peases was one of the more uncomfortable dealings I've had in my life. We had some second thoughts about moving here, I must tell you."

Pete looked at Evelyn's bandage. He could imagine

another woman would be having some pretty strong third thoughts about it right now.

"Here, I'll copy down this information for you. Unfortunately, I think they take their time on the way down, and I have no further information about destinations en route. It's funny. I'm sure it must have been something we did that set those Peases off wrong, but I can't imagine what it is."

"You bought a piece of property he had to sell but couldn't bear to sell, and now he blames you for it. Nashtoba logic."

Evelyn Waxman's grin looked ghoulish under all that gauze. "You wait and see. I'll wear the old coot down yet!"

Pete looked again at the long list of signatures on the petition. He was sure she would.

The phone number Evelyn Waxman gave Pete connected him to a condominium office in Boca Raton, where he was told that the Peases were not expected for a week. Pete gave up on the M-1 and headed for Jerry's barn.

By four o'clock the framing was done. Pete climbed down from the roof and waded into the white pine forest, ax in hand.

It was dark in the woods. For once the air was still. Pete stood in the silent heart of the forest and thought winter thoughts that probably dated all the way back to the old country and the Druids, sure that if he waited long enough something hidden in these woods would answer all his questions, would tell him just what to do.

A twig snapped someplace and Pete shook himself out of his daze. He moved off through the woods searching for just the right-size pine and finally found it—a seedling that was crowding its neighbor and about to be strangled in woodbine. He cracked into it with the ax, slung it over his shoulder, and returned to the barn.

Pete fixed the little pine to the ridgepole of the newly framed barn, a tradition that was older than the island itself, intended to honor the wood from which the barn would grow.

He was just climbing down from the roof for the second time when Connie's dark green sports car with the scarred black leather top pulled into Jerry's drive.

Chapter
10

Connie leaned back into her car to collect the school assignment she brought for Jill Beggs, one of her students who had been out sick the day before. True, there were others who could have brought the work to Jill, and true, she wasn't exactly surprised to find Pete still here working on Jerry's barn . . . Connie fidgeted around at an awkward angle until she couldn't in good conscience fiddle around anymore, backed out of the tiny car, whirled around, and smacked right into Pete.

"Whoa!" Pete grabbed her arm to steady her and she dropped her books. They bent down together, scrambling in the pine needles to pick them up.

"I'm sorry," said Connie.

Pete looked up and stayed looking. "*I'm* sorry."

Was there supposed to be some extra meaning here? Was the air finally going to get cleared? Maybe. But there was something about the way Pete said *his* sorry, something that made *his* sound like a generous gift and *hers* sound like interest on an overdue bill.

Connie jumped up, hugging her books to the knot in her chest, but suddenly something about that pose in combination with their conversation made it all seem so high-schoolish that she started to laugh.

At once Pete's even teeth flashed in answer.

Hell. She wasn't about to split hairs here, and besides, maybe she'd imagined it. Connie took a deep breath of the freshened air and tried again. "So! Barn's all framed? Trademark tree is up? You're off to celebrate?"

"Do you want to? Lupo's for a beer?"

Connie was so surprised at the question that it took her a second to answer, and in that one second Pete almost took it all back.

"But it's Friday. You're busy. Going out, I guess."

Connie knew a test question when she heard one, but she'd been known to ace an occasional test in her day. "I'm not doing a damned thing. Lupo's for a beer it is." Without waiting to see if Pete registered her response with relief or panic she strode over to his truck, hopped in, and landed smack on top of an empty Coke bottle. That took care of the conversation for a minute or two. After that she babbled on nervously all the way to the bar.

The minute they walked into Lupo's a kind of hush seemed to fall. Real or imaginary, Connie wasn't sure, but she *was* sure she saw a few eyebrows go up. She should have expected it. On this island this was big news—Pete and Connie Bartholomew out for a beer! Pete led them toward a booth, but once they were actually facing each other silence descended, and the voices at the bar seemed very loud. And drunk.

"Only mistake I made was not walking out on her sooner," said Abel Cobb. "It gets so you got to live a little, check out those greener pastures. Always are greener, too—don't believe it when they say they aren't!"

Across the booth from Connie, Pete's face froze.

Wally Melville and Abel Cobb exited the bar with raucous laughter. The silence in their own booth clung.

Pete found Tina Hansey, the waitress, and ordered Connie's favorite beer, Ballantine Ale. Connie, ready at all times to meet someone halfway, countered with Pete's favorite subject: murder.

"So what does the chief think these days? Does he think there's any connection between Newby Dillingham and Evelyn Waxman? Does he think one person tried to kill them both? If someone *did* try to kill Evelyn?"

Pete perked up. "Yeah, the chief thinks someone tried to kill her."

"He thinks the same person tried both?"

"I don't think he wants to think there might be two nuts around here. But the only connection I can make is the condo one. Newby didn't want to sell, and Evelyn certainly didn't want him to. The whole island knows how those two felt."

"And what's with this old bullet? Does that mean the chief's only considering World War Two vets and older?"

"World War Two vets are at least in their sixties by now, don't forget," said Pete, warming up nicely now. "And most World War One vets are dead."

"They won't be the only ones if this keeps up," said Connie. It was supposed to be a joke, but Pete unsettled her by taking it otherwise.

"That's what worries me," said Pete. "That's why the chief's looking for a connection, so he can head off whatever's next."

"Condos," repeated Connie. "So who wanted the sale? Nate Cox. And Ozzie, of course, that son of a bitch."

Connie could feel herself heating up just thinking about Ozzie. Pete looked at her curiously. Not that anyone should need to explain why they didn't like Ozzie around here, but still, Connie knew, the intensity of her reaction probably did call for an explanation of sorts.

"I capsized in the hotel's catamaran last summer. I couldn't get it back up. There I was, upside down over the top pontoon, when Ozzie motored in close, told me to stop waving my ass in his face because he wasn't that hard up, and went on by! I could have killed him!"

Pete laughed, but it sounded kind of sweaty and tired, sort of the way Connie was starting to feel. She supposed this was normal, all this conversational strain, but it had never been like this the *first* time they dated. Of course the first time Connie hadn't had the San Andreas fault to contend with and an ex-husband sitting there silently waiting for her to dig herself out or fall back in. So okay. So she could handle this. She struggled on, avoiding dangerous subjects like their relationship and sticking to benign ones like murder.

"And look at Nate Cox. I hear he's just about set up a roadblock in front of that house on Shore Road he's been trying to sell."

Pete didn't seem to want to talk about Nate. "There is another connection besides the condos. The Dillinghams and the Waxmans both ended up with Pease land."

Connie grabbed at yet another conversational straw even while disgusted at how quickly she jumped in to defame a fellow islander. "You mean maybe Cyrus decided he'd been gypped out of his land and took revenge?"

"Whether or not Cyrus got gypped is a matter of interpretation. Besides, Cyrus left for Florida before the shooting at Beston's Store. I guess it's not much of a connection."

"I guess not. Everyone's connected around here anyhow, by land, by blood, by marriage."

As Connie said the word *marriage* she could see Pete's jaws clench just the way her mother's used to when Connie used a four-letter word. Connie's steam finally left her. She drained her beer and fumbled in her knapsack for her money.

"Hey," said Pete. "*I* asked. I pay."

Connie let him, too exhausted to argue.

She got up, and Pete followed without a word.

It was pitch black when they got back to the Beggs house. They wouldn't have been able to see Jerry at all if he hadn't been tangled up in the string of Christmas lights he had apparently wound around Pete's little pine before the sniper shot him down.

They moved without speaking, each with the efficiency that comes with massive infusions of adrenaline. Connie catapulted out of the truck, Pete angled his headlights on the scene, and Jerry's face sprang up at Connie white as death, his shoulder soggy and black. "Oh, Christ," she whispered.

Jerry rolled his head to the side and moaned.

Connie shot up. "He's not dead!" She tore off for the house and phone.

Through the glass panes in the kitchen door she could see a wall phone, and Connie didn't bother to knock. She crashed into the kitchen hollering "Betsy!" only later wondering if some sort of tact should have been applied, but she had already connected to the police station when Betsy came clattering down the stairs. "There's been a shooting," she hollered into the phone at Ted. "We need an ambulance at the Beggs place. It looks like a shoulder wound, anyway, I don't know what else. And a bad fall."

Extra words did not have to be said. Betsy, the solid, sensible, corduroy type, pushed past Connie and outside.

*   *   *

Pete stood next to Connie on the brown winter grass and watched what was fast becoming a familiar scene: the doors of the ambulance closing behind a fully loaded stretcher.

"He's not dead," Connie said for the twelfth time. "Thank God he's not dead."

"He'll be okay," said Pete, also, he was sure, for the twelfth time.

The ambulance pulled away with Betsy's white face looking stoically straight ahead from the passenger seat, her daughter Jill peering anxiously from the window of the bedroom to which she had been sent. Willy McOwat returned to Pete and Connie.

"So you left here at what time?" he asked, and Pete took the chief through their timetable of the evening, surprised to find it was still so early. Lupo's seemed years ago, and he could have sworn Connie had dropped her books in the Beggses' drive a couple of years before that. He looked at Connie now and saw that same look of strained fatigue he had seen on her face at Sarah's. Pete knew that look, knew it always followed the first of Connie's two speeds, full steam ahead, and preceded the second of her speeds, total collapse. He wasn't sure she could keep standing there much longer.

The police moved away toward the woods.

"Let me drive you home," said Pete. "It's not far— I can walk back for the truck."

Connie shook her head no at the same time that she handed over the keys and moved toward the passenger side of her car.

All during the short ride Pete tried to think of something to say that would resurrect the night's hopeful start, that would keep it from ending in a nightmare.

It was Connie who finally did it, right at her door, with two simple words. "Don't go."

Pete followed her up the stairs.

Isn't this crazy, Pete thought a good hour later, Jerry's been shot, and here we sit talking about Christmas. Was that what fear did? Or was it something else? He could feel the heat of her body beside him, could sense her conspiring along with him to push away the horrors of the night, the months, the years. Suddenly it seemed he could say anything to her, ask anything of her, have his every expectation met in response.

"So those are your choices, Florida or Maine?" she asked.

"Or I can stay here." Pete leaned forward and twisted a little so he could see her face, to see if she knew what he meant. Yes, she knew.

"I'm supposed to go to New Jersey, but you know what that's like."

Pete grinned. The grin felt new on his face, a grin free of the old uncertainty and fear. Christmas with Connie. It was only twelve days away. He poked the papier-mâché Santa perched on the coffee table so that the large head on the end of a long spring waggled. The Santa wobbled and fell, the head rolled onto the floor, and suddenly Pete was reminded of Jerry. What was the matter with him? Jerry had been shot, and here Pete sat feeling full of . . . full of *Christmas*.

Connie picked up the Santa head, all of a sudden looking a little more pasty herself.

"He'll be all right," said Pete. "I'll go see him in the morning."

"But why Jerry? He doesn't have anything to do with the condos. He's not living on Pease land."

Pete shook his head. "That's the thing about all this. Who'd hurt Jerry? *Or* Newby or Evelyn. If you tried to think of the three people least likely to hurt a fly, there they'd be. Jerry, Newby, Evelyn. I don't know of any connection between Jerry and the Peases at all. And I don't see where the condos fit in.''

"They *don't* fit in. Not around here. Christ.''

"Evelyn Waxman told me Cyrus has rented a condo in Florida. I can't even picture *that*. Of course he isn't *in* the condo in Florida yet. I don't know *where* he is. I wish I did.''

"Glen might know where he is.''

Glen. The name of the man she had run away with dropped on Pete's ears like a bomb. *Glen?*

"I mean, if it's important for you to find him, Glen might be able to tell you.''

"How's that?'' asked Pete carefully, coolly.

"Cyrus and Glen are related. Cousins or something. I thought you knew that.''

"No,'' said Pete. "I didn't.''

"Well, they are.'' Connie sounded a little snappish. "We just got through saying everyone's related to everyone around here.''

"I thought Glen was in California.''

"He moved back east about a month ago. He's over on the Hook. Naushon.''

And that was that. Pete's short-lived euphoria drained out of him like the helium out of a balloon. She was still in touch with Glen.

"So, you're saying if I wanted Cyrus's whereabouts you could get it for me from Glen.''

"I'm saying if you want *Glen's* address I can give it to you, and you can get Cyrus's whereabouts yourself.''

"I see.''

The ice in the air was now close to visible. "Do you want the address or not?'' Connie almost shouted.

"Yes.''

Connie jumped up, found her knapsack, and rummaged through it until she resurfaced with a crumpled envelope. She fished in again and came out with paper and pen. She scrawled Glen's address on the piece of paper, retaining the envelope, Pete noticed, while she shoved the paper at Pete.

Pete was now standing near the door.

"Thank you."

"You're welcome."

There was nothing more to say. Pete walked toward the door feeling like he'd sat on a poker.

Connie turned and kicked the smiling, wagging Santa across the floor.

Chapter

11

Pete drove to Sarah Abrew's the next morning to read her the paper, as he had being doing off and on for twenty years, but he was so enmeshed in his own hair shirt of thoughts that he missed the turn to her house.

Would he never learn? He'd sat beside Connie thinking how much he had missed this—being close to a person, talking, almost believing they could learn to treasure each other again. The next thing he knew she was jotting off an address that was not a month old. She was still in touch with Glen.

Pete turned the truck around, listening to the radio blab on about the ten more shopping days till Christmas. So who cared? At Sarah's the Mormon Tabernacle Choir was squawking again, this time "Angels We Have Heard on High." Pete strode across her living room and shut off the tape.

"Well, Merry Christmas to you, too," Sarah snapped.

"Do you want to listen to the paper or do you want to listen to that? Take your pick."

Sarah peered at him from behind her thick lenses.

"In the mood you're in you'd better start with the obits."

Pete crashed onto the couch and snapped open the paper. A sketchy account of the shooting of Jerry Beggs was the lead story. Pete read it off fast. Somehow the rest of the news seemed superfluous after that, and he stopped reading at all, lost in thought. Jerry had been shot. Cyrus had left for Florida. That left Nate Cox or Ozzie Dillingham?

As if she were reading his mind, Sarah asked, "Ozzie hasn't sold out yet?"

"I don't know."

"And Jerry's all right?"

"I don't know that either. I'm going to the hospital from here."

"Well, don't walk in on him looking like that. He'll think you just ran into the undertaker coming down hall."

Pete stood up, annoyed. Couldn't he have one day where he wasn't expected to be everyone's good humor man all the time? "I'll see you tomorrow," he said, but Sarah was having none of that.

"Get over here!"

Pete got. Sarah grabbed his hand, pulled him down, and peered into his face.

"What's the matter with you?"

"Nothing's the matter with me. Just because a friend of mine has been shot, just because I don't want to hear the same dumb songs hour after hour, day after day, year after year—"

"Well, all I can say is I hope my Joanna's in a better mood for Christmas than you are."

Pete straightened up, feeling suddenly and unreasonably abandoned. "You're going to your daughter's?"

"If Joanna has her way I'm taking the train to Baltimore the Monday before and coming home the Monday after. Foolishness. Her spending all the money and me traipsing all that way for just a week.''

The voice was crabbed but there was a flush of excitement in the cheeks that didn't fool Pete. God only knew why, but after eighty-six years of this drivel Sarah Abrew still loved Christmas. And she did enjoy seeing her daughter. *Once* in a while.

"Let me know when—I'll get you to the station.''

"If I go. I still have eleven days to decide.''

"If you go.'' He turned once again for the door and then hesitated. "Hey, Sarah.''

"What?''

"Cyrus Pease. He's related to Glen Newcomb?''

The half-blind eyes looked at him way too sharply. "Now let me see. Yes, he would be. Cyrus's father and Glen's grandmother were brother and sister. Glen's mother was Cyrus's first cousin. What does that make Glen and Cyrus—second cousins? First cousins once removed? I never did know how those cousins worked. Why?''

"No reason.''

"Glen's still in California?''

"No,'' said Pete. "He isn't. He's in Naushon.''

"Naushon! What's he doing there?''

"Old fish never die, they just hang around and stink a lot.''

Sarah peered at Pete. "On second thought, maybe you'd better stay here. I don't think Jerry can survive your presence so soon after being shot.''

Pete thought of giving Sarah's door a good slam but he decided not to give her that satisfaction.

Bradford Hospital was not one of Pete's favorite places, especially since he spent the past summer in it recovering from a complicated knife wound incurred when he had jumped between a man's fist and a woman's face. It's the bareness of the walls, he thought, the bareness of the floors, as if they expect you to spurt blood all over them. Pete pounded up the stairs to the second floor and Jerry's nurse's station. When he heard that Jerry had had the good sense to refuse all visitors except his wife, he turned away with relief only to run smack into Betsy coming out of the room.

"Pete. I'm glad you're here. Jerry wants to talk to you. The shoulder wound isn't too bad but they're more concerned about the fall. He's cracked a couple of ribs and they're keeping him one more night to observe him for internal injuries." Betsy shivered in front of Pete and pushed open the hospital room door. Pete took a deep breath and felt an immediate pain in the site of his old injury. What if he started bleeding? What if they wouldn't let him leave?

Jerry was sitting up in bed with masses of stark white bandages around his shoulder and stark white sheets around the rest of him. He was about Pete's age, but today he looked gray and fifty. He peered over the half-glasses that Pete had always suspected he affected for the bookstore-owner image he felt he needed to project. Pete was surprised to see him actually using them to read the paper.

"Jer!"

"So what happened?"

Pete looked behind him at Betsy, but she just nodded at her husband in the bed.

"You're asking me?"

"Betsy said you found me lying out there on the ground. What happened?"

"Connie and I had gone to Lupo's for a beer. When we came back to pick up her car, there you were on the ground. You couldn't have been there long."

"He hadn't been outside for half an hour," said Betsy, outraged, as if a half hour's absence shouldn't

101

be long enough in which to get shot. "When he got home and saw the little tree he put some Christmas lights on it. Then later, after it got dark, he didn't like the way it looked, and went back out to adjust them. I told you, Jerry, it was a pretty foolish thing to do in the dark."

Jerry rolled his eyes. "I don't remember anything. I sort of remember being on the roof and fiddling with the lights and hearing something. A thud. I thought it was a bulb. I didn't even feel it—not really, not at first. Then I spun around and lost my balance and fell."

"I didn't hear a thing," said Betsy. "I was upstairs with Jill—you know how she's been coughing. The next thing I heard was Connie charging into the house."

I bet, thought Pete.

"Didn't you see anything?" asked Jerry.

"Only you on the ground, trailing a string of Christmas lights. After the police came and the ambulance took you away I left." Pete remembered Connie lifting her chin the way she did when she was pulling out all stops to hold herself together. That was why he'd left so fast, but that wasn't the way he explained it to the Beggses. "It wasn't like at Beston's. There had been some elapsed time since the shot, and no one clear place it must have come from."

Jerry thought for a minute. "True. I tell you, I may not be God's gift, but I'm damned if I can figure out who'd want to shoot me."

Pete couldn't figure it either. Even if the condo deal was the underlying motivation for all these shootings, where did Jerry fit in with that? He ran a bookstore that could only benefit from more tourist trade, and judging by his Christmas push he was pretty aggressive about his plans for success. True, he'd signed Evelyn's petition, but he hadn't been outspoken about the issue. As a matter of fact, he had diplomatically not talked about it at all.

"You don't figure into the condo issue," said Pete out loud.

"Oh, I don't know," said Betsy. "Nate Cox has been pestering you to sign a lease on the mini-mall they're planning to go along with it."

Jerry waved a dismissive hand. "The mall's only going in if Nate can get enough leasers to commit up front. I'm staying on Main Street. He just doesn't believe me yet."

"The man's a pest! He kept calling, kept trying to get you to commit to a move. Finally you had a few words, didn't you, Jerry?"

Jerry frowned. "Not words, exactly. I told him in a jocular way that I would consider any further calls harassment and that the authorities would be notifed if he bothered me again. I didn't mean it."

"He thought you did, though. He got all worked up. He never came back, either. You should have told the chief when he came again this morning. You should tell him, Jerry."

Jerry continued to frown. He didn't look so terrific in general, and Pete didn't figure the conversation was helping things much.

"I'm going to the station next. I'll fill them in if you want."

Jerry's face brightened. "If you think it means anything. Personally I don't, but that chief seemed somewhat disgruntled that I wasn't more help." Suddenly Jerry grinned. "But I'm a lot more help than Newby! He should thank me for that, at least!"

There was a funny noise beside Pete. He turned to find Betsy gulping back sobs from behind clenched fists.

"Aw, love," said Jerry, holding out his good arm, and Betsy charged forward and fell onto him.

Jerry winced.

At the police station Jean Martell was so pumped full of tidbits that she had some trouble getting her mouth open to spit them out. Preliminary examination showed all three bullets appeared to match. Not that Pete had doubted it, not that on his worst day could he imagine more than one nut shooting around the island at one time. Although in his present mood he could almost do a little sniping himself. At certain targets. Paul and Ted were nowhere in sight. Jean tried to pump Pete about his and Connie's presence at the shooting, almost as big a news item as the shooting itself, but she gave up in the face of his string of monosyllables. She finally gave an imperial wave that directed Pete down the hall to the chief.

Willy was clearly not getting much sleep. His face was draped with shadows and his usually square shoulders seemed to droop. He rubbed a hand over his face and Pete was pretty sure he snuck in a yawn behind it.

"Did you find out anything about CRAP?"

"I found out they're under a lot of pressure. The financing won't wait. They have thirty days to sign or they're back to square one."

Pete mulled that over. He then told him about Nate Cox pressuring Jerry to sign a lease for the mall. He also told him about Buck Bacon's M-1 being sold to Cyrus Pease, and then he hesitated. He could hand over Glen Newcomb's address and be done with it, but suddenly, finally, perversely, he was in a mood to talk to Glen Newcomb himself. He decided to stall. Instead he asked the chief about the bullet Jack Whiteaker had found.

"So what about nine millimeter bullets—are those legal for hunting?"

"Depends what you're hunting. That's what we use."

"The one Jack Whiteaker found was one of yours?"

Willy frowned. *"What* one Jack Whiteaker found?"

"The one I gave to Paul. He said it was nine-millimeter. He put it in his pocket."

The chief rose slowly from behind his desk, and Pete sensed a storm pending. He decided he'd better get his own agenda lined up now.

"I might be able to get you Cyrus Pease's address. He's Glen Newcomb's cousin or something. Glen's on the Hook—I was planning to talk to him today."

Willy looked at Pete. Contrary to what the rest of the island thought, the chief was pretty good at figuring things out. "Now?"

"Now." This particular dead fish had been stinking up the place long enough.

It was one of his longer treks over the causeway to the Hook, and on the ride Pete thought not of what he was going to say to Glen Newcomb, but what exactly it was that had upset him so about Connie last night. He had spent a long year trying to convince himself that it was over. Finally he had realized there was more to be said, and last night they had seemed on the verge of saying some of it. What went wrong? Glen. Or more accurately, Connie's possession of Glen's current address. Pete had never deluded himself that he and Connie could end up friends. It was going to have to be all or nothing, and Connie's having Glen's new address put things far from the "all" end of the scale.

Pete didn't blame Glen. After all, Connie had admitted that the whole thing had been her idea, that she had snapped up Glen as her ticket out, had wrecked two marriages without a backward glance. No, Pete didn't hold any animosity toward Glen. True, Glen had been working at Factotum along with Pete and Connie at the time, and Pete had considered him his friend. Still, Pete knew that you had to be made of steel to withstand Connie when she was under a full head of steam. No, he didn't blame Glen.

Pete was therefore surprised to find that his first impulse, when he saw Glen on the other side of the threshold, was to put his fist straight through his glasses and into his face.

Neither of them spoke.

Neither of them looked too happy, either.

"Well," said Glen finally. "Fancy finding you here."

Pete shoved his balled-up fists into his pockets. He had hoped he was over his short-lived and highly ineffective aggressive stage.

"Police business," said Pete, and Glen raised an eyebrow, as well he might. "We're looking for your cousin Cyrus Pease. He's left for Florida but isn't due there for a week and Connie thinks you might know his itinerary in between."

Glen's tall, skinny body didn't move from the middle of the doorway, and he blinked at Pete from behind his thick lenses. "You came over here to find out about my cousin? Connie told you where I was?"

Pete nodded.

The magnified eyes behind the glasses looked extremely puzzled, and Pete could see why. By now even Pete didn't know why he was there.

"Well," said Glen, "I think I'm going to want to hear why you're looking for Cyrus before I say much else. Do you want to tell me about it out there or in here?"

He stood to one side. Against his better judgment, Pete stepped across the threshold and into the room.

When Glen Newcomb and his wife, Abby, had lived

106

together on Nashtoba, they had lived in an apartment that had been one of those not-a-hair-out-of-place types. For some reason Pete had always assumed that the closely clipped Abby was responsible for that look—now he could clearly see that it must have been Glen. Each white wall of Glen's apartment held a perfectly centered, black-framed photograph of a seascape. The two chairs and one couch were cheap Sears Roebuck but matching and meticulously maintained. The polished coffee table held three sailing magazines, each one equally spaced from the other and centered on the table. Pete wondered how Glen had reacted to the way Connie discarded her clothes on the floor.

"Coffee?"

Pete shook his head, but Glen left the room for it anyway. As soon as he was gone Pete picked up one of the sailing magazines and threw it back down out of line with its neighbor.

When Glen reentered the room he carried a tray that held a coffee carafe, two cups, a bottle of Wild Turkey, and two glasses.

Glen Newcomb reached for the Wild Turkey. Pete, who had hoped that his short-lived but indiscriminate drinking phase was also at an end, held up a glass.

"So what do you want with Cyrus?"

For a minute Pete couldn't remember who Cyrus was. He gulped the whiskey and reveled in the burn. Cyrus. "You know about the sniper?"

Glen nodded. He hadn't once removed his eyes from Pete. Was he worried that Pete was going to take a potshot at *him?*

"The sniper's using old military ammunition and presumably an old military rifle. Rumor has it that your uncle bought the M-1 that Buck Bacon smuggled home from the war. The cops want to make sure he still has it."

"And that he hasn't used it?"

Pete shrugged. He didn't add that they knew Cyrus was an old hand at the military shoots. "They just want to get hold of Cyrus. This just seemed the easiest way."

Glen laughed. It sounded bitter. "For whom? Come on, Pete. What do you want, an apology? An explanation? Okay, here it is. God knows I've spent enough time trying to think one up. Okay. I flirted shamelessly with your wife, for no other reason than I figured she was the safest person around. Much to my surprise she called my bluff—I'm still not sure I know just why. We had one fast, furious fling that day we were working in the Blakes' house, and the next thing I know Connie's talking about leaving town. Didn't want to face you, I guess."

Glen paused. "I wasn't too sorry to get out of there. Abby and I didn't get along for beans. Connie, though— she wasn't even halfway over the causeway when she knew she'd made a mistake. It took her a little longer to admit it, that's all."

Pete didn't speak.

"Look. I'm not sorry for what it did to my marriage. I *am* sorry for what it did to yours. I'm also sorry she left me. Okay?"

Pete closed his eyes, set down his drink. *No, not okay.*

Glen assessed Pete in silence for a second. "You know, I told her you'd never take her back. I guess she knew you better."

Still Pete said nothing.

"Is that why you came here—to show me you'd won?"

Pete stood up. "I haven't won anything. If you have that address—"

"I have Cyrus's address in Florida, but I don't know

where he might have stopped on the way. I do know his guns aren't with him. I have his keys. I'll make a deal with you. I'll go back over with you, go in with you, check out his guns with you.''

"And?"

Glen turned away. "And nothing. That's it.''

"I wouldn't know an M-1 if I fell over it.''

"I would."

They drove in separate cars back to Nashtoba, to Cyrus Pease's farm.

The farmhouse itself was locked. The room in which Cyrus kept all his guns was also locked, but Glen had keys for both. He opened the door to the back room and from floor to ceiling along the walls and in cases on every table and chest were guns.

Glen walked without hesitation to a glass case on top of a three-drawer dresser, selected yet another key, and unlocked the case. "This is Buck's Garand.''

He removed the gun and held it out to Pete.

"I don't think you should be touching it. I'll have to get the police over here. Is it loaded?''

"Always assume a gun is loaded.''

"Is it?"

"Of course not."

"Stop handling it," said Pete, thinking partly of fingerprints, and partly that he just wanted him to put the damned thing down. Pete left the room, found the phone, called the police station, and got Paul Roose.

Paul arrived alone. He spent a long time examining all the guns. Finally he picked up the Garand and clicked it through its paces, looking it over inside and out. Apparently Paul didn't much care about fingerprints either.

"Why didn't Cyrus pilfer his own M-1 back in forty-five?'' Paul asked.

"Why didn't you pilfer yours?" Glen answered.

Paul grinned. He gave Glen a receipt for it, shoved it into a long canvas case he'd brought along, and left.

Pete and Glen didn't speak further, only saying a tight good-bye at their cars. As Pete headed home the truck radio suddenly blasted into "White Christmas."

It started to rain.

Again.

Chapter
12

"Then I'll stay here alone!" Maxine shouted at her mother. "If I can't stay with Dad I'll just stay here alone! It's *your* stupid aunt Ethel."

"It's your great-aunt Ethel," Rita reminded her daughter, against her better judgment. "And she's looking forward to seeing you. She's expecting you to be there."

"Well, you'll just have to unexpect her!"

"No," said Rita, suddenly fed up. "*You'll* have to. And you're not staying anywhere alone. If you're not going, make your own arrangements, then call Aunt Ethel yourself and tell her you won't be there." Rita Peck turned away from her daughter in disgust, but only after Maxine turned away from *her* in disgust, and Rita returned to the phone.

"It was a *hissling* sound!" Mrs. Potts was saying. "I tell you, it knocked down my wreath and went right into the woods! Where *is* he? I want Pete to come over and look in the woods! I just *know* that bullet's in there! He found the other bullet in such a clever way. I'm sure he'll find this one. You do know how desperately the police need these clues."

111

Maxine slammed the door behind her. Rita Peck held the phone away from her ear and rubbed her aching lobe. "Mrs. Potts, Pete is not here. Again, I think you should inform the police."

Mrs. Potts tsk-tsked into the phone. "Rita, I told you. I don't want to bother the *police*—not with a murderer running loose. Just have Pete run over as soon as—"

"Pete will not be back until late. If you don't call the police right now I will do so myself."

There was a horrified silence on the other end of the phone. *"Really,"* said Mrs. Potts. "I mean really. If you're *sure*—"

"I'm sure," said Rita, and she hung up the phone.

"Lordy," she said to Andy, who had just burst into the room. She scanned her desk quickly for any precarious or breakable items. "This is getting out of hand. That's the third report we've had of a sniper. Imagine what the police must be getting."

"They've issued a warning," said Andy. "They want everyone to keep their curtains pulled at night, to keep away from lighted windows. The whole place is going crazy." He rummaged in his pocket and pulled out a small, coppery tube of metal, placing it on Rita's desk. "The Meechams gave me this to bring to Pete. They found it in their woods and they think it's from the sniper's gun."

"What *is* it?" asked Rita.

"Cartridge casing," said Allison, who had slipped up to the desk unheard and unnoticed. "But it's not the sniper's—it's from a twenty-two."

Andy rumpled up Allison's white straws of hair. "Hey, scarecrow. What's up? Your dad drag this place into the twentieth century yet?"

Allison ducked from under Andy's hands and whipped around on him, her voice as quiet as ever but somehow frightening in its very control. "My father was home

112

with me and my mother the night of the party, the night of the carols, the night at the Beggses'."

"Hey!" said Andy. "I didn't mean anything! I just meant did he sell the condos yet? Jeeze, Allie!"

"And what business of yours is that?"

Pete opened the door behind Allison but she didn't seem to hear or see him. She was busy expending what was for her an entire day's worth of words. "The ballistics tests on my father's gun did not match up to the bullets. Now the police are searching our house. I'm sure everyone will be glad to know the strategy's working. My parents are talking about leaving town."

"That's not true," said Pete, and Allison whirled around. "Nobody's trying to get your father to move. But let's be a little realistic here. Your father's a World War Two veteran, he's an expert marksman, he stands to gain by the sale of the bait shop. The police are doing their job."

Allison's face mottled an unbecoming purple. "My father may be a World War Two veteran but he's no expert marksman. He spent that war behind a desk."

Pete looked doubtful.

Allison's expression had a little *Et tu, Brute* in it in return.

Rita looked at Allison more closely, and all of a sudden there was something about her mooning around the office of late that Rita didn't like.

Coincidentally, it was right about then that Rita began to wonder if maybe Connie's coming back wasn't so bad after all.

Connie took the quickest route down Shore Road to Main Street to Hansey's, Nashtoba's one clothing store—a sensible sort of store that augmented its timeless classics with rubber boots and foul weather gear—trying to catch it before it closed. The obligatory teacher's Christmas party required a dress, and a dress was something that Connie's closet no longer offered. Over the past year she had put on a pound or two. Not enough to bother her much, not something that wouldn't go away as soon as she stopped eating all the time, but still, it was enough so that her stock party dress was too tight in the waist, and Connie refused to walk around all night unable to breathe.

On Shore Road Connie passed Pete's truck but he didn't see her, or at least if he did he didn't wave, but drove on scowling at the road. Behind Pete's truck was a silver Toyota that she knew less well, but a second look confirmed her initial surprise. Glen Newcomb. She slowed and scanned her rearview mirror. First Pete's truck and then Glen's Toyota turned off Shore Road into Pease's farm.

Pete *and* Glen. So giving him that address must have paid off for someone, if not for her. The fact that she even had Glen's address was so ironic. A long-overdue rebate check had finally come, Glen had mailed it on to her at her old address at Factotum, and someone—it must have been Rita—had quietly forwarded it on to Pease Street. Connie had read Glen's brief note and marked his return to Naushon with little interest and only slight trepidation. She and Glen had been over and done with before they started and both of them knew it. Why the *hell* had she offered the address to Pete?

Connie entered Hansey's in a daze. The first and only thing she tried on was a soft gray wool dress that looked straight and plain on the hanger. She tossed it on and kept it there only long enough to make sure that it didn't scratch, tug, cut, or constrict her in any way. She had other things on her mind. She bought it. She made three more stops that gleaned the last six Christmas gifts she had yet to buy and returned home.

As soon as Connie walked in the door the telephone

rang. Connie hated it when the phone rang the minute she walked in. It always made her think of disasters and dead people, and relatives so anxious to pass on bad news they kept calling and calling until she walked in the door. Or was it some psycho lurking and waiting and *watching* until she walked in? Connie couldn't see the point in postponing bad news. She marched to the phone and picked it up.

"Hello!"

"Ah," said a once-familiar voice.

Connie said nothing.

"You flashed back into my mind today in a most curious way. Your ex-husband paid me a call. I thought he was going to shoot me. I thought he was the now-famous island sniper, come for his real target after all."

"Are you drunk?"

"I think so. Are you?"

"No," said Connie, who had sworn off Ballantine Ales as of the first thing Sunday morning.

"Too bad. You were always more fun drunk. You talked yourself into so many stupid things when you were drunk—like running away with me."

Connie said nothing.

"I'm calling to see if you feel like talking yourself into it again. I got the feeling from your ex-husband you weren't back with him after all. I decided you were worth one more good try. Wanna?"

"No."

"You mean you're not going to make it so easy this time? You mean *I* have to talk *you* into it? Or do I have to get even more drastic than that?"

"It was drastic enough last time. What did you tell him? Doesn't he know that it wasn't—"

"Wasn't what? Oh, it wasn't a lot, I grant you, but is was *something*. It was *enough*. You don't really expect him to forget about it, do you? Just because *you* can forget it doesn't mean everyone else can, you know.''

Suddenly, and to her horror, Connie felt her eyes fill up with tears. "I haven't forgotten a damned thing, Glen! And I don't expect anybody to forget anything! I just don't happen to think I should have to go on paying for this for—" She choked to a stop.

"Wait a minute, that's not you *crying*, is it? Oh, Connie, save your tears—you're going to need them later."

Connie slammed down the phone, sat on the floor, and cried. She didn't allow herself to cry too often and she wasn't very good at it—it sounded like someone was strangling a goose.

Chapter
13

Christmas was closing in. Pete could tell by the way the drunks at the bar were tuning up. He tried to tune them out, and turned back to Willy.

"So Cyrus Pease's gun was clean."

"Recently cleaned. Not necessarily the same thing. The lab is doing ballistics testing. Now about Newcomb."

Newcomb. He kept dragging Pete back to it, with an insistence that was beginning to wear on Pete. What was his point here? Was he trying to prove he was still the friend as well as the chief? Pete didn't need this kind of proof. The chief may not have been an islander but he was still a New England and had, up until now, anyway, possessed that healthy New England trait of keeping himself to himself, and leaving Pete to Pete.

"You say you went to Glen Newcomb's today and he returned with you to Cyrus's?"

Pete took Willy through the pertinent parts of his day with Glen Newcomb again, a day that had drained him of every last ounce of steam. It had only been the insistent, haunted look in the chief's eyes that had dragged him out at ten o'clock tonight at all, and now he was sorry he had come. The chief kept *squinting* at him all the time. Pete took a solid slug of beer at the end of his recital, grasped the wheel of the conversation and turned it.

"Well, how about Cyrus? He's out of it now, isn't he, since he'd left before Jerry got shot?"

"Since we can't find Cyrus yet, we don't know if he's gone, or if he is, how far away he's gotten. I checked at the Gun Club and he's a fair shot with those old weapons at the military shoots. Nothing earth-shattering, but fair."

"But still, Cyrus must be out of it. Despite the Pease-Dillingham-Waxman land thing, Jerry Beggs throws a—"

The chief snapped up straighter. "What Pease-Waxman land thing?"

Pete told him about the Waxmans buying Pease's land. The chief's beer mug started to steam up.

"And Beggs? Now you're going to tell me Beggs bought his place from—"

"Jerry doesn't have anything to do with Cyrus—not that I can figure, anyway. I can't see where Jerry has anything to do with Newby or Evelyn. I'm not even convinced someone was trying to kill Jerry. It was pitch black. How could anyone have seen him on that roof?"

Willy shook his head impatiently. "Beggs had everything to do with Newby and Evelyn. All three bullets match. There must be a thread here—there must be some connection among all three shootings. And he must be aiming to kill because he's not missing by much. One too many beers might have been the only difference between missing Waxman, winging Beggs, killing Dillingham." At the word *beers* Willy looked with distaste at the usual commotion at Lupo's bar, where Wally Melville and Abel Cobb were competing loudly for the attentions of the waitress, Tina Hansey.

"So what about Nate Cox and the condo connection

among all three?" Pete suddenly remembered Allison and started to feel guilty that he'd brought Nate Cox up. "But you searched his house and didn't find anything, I hear."

"No, we didn't. But you have to look at it this way. A murderer isn't going to leave the weapon lying around. He's going to get rid of it if he's through with it. He's going to hide it if he isn't."

"But do you think the sniper's through with it?"

"He'll be through with it if I get him before he uses it again."

Somehow that wasn't the most reassuring thought. Pete sipped his beer morosely. "What about all these miscellaneous reports of snipers? Is there anything in any of that?"

"These miscellaneous reports are all coming from flakes. I've worn out the required shoe leather tracking them down, but I think we can pretty safely say that these shootings are going to fit a certain pattern. They'll be restricted to night; they'll be from a range of around a hundred yards, which is clearly this fellow's best distance; and they'll be from an old military rifle."

"Alibis, then? You don't seem impressed with Nate Cox's."

"Provided by his wife and daughter? You think I should be?"

"She says he can't shoot. She says he sat behind a desk the whole war." Pete said it tentatively. He was still worried about Allison. *Something* about Allison.

"Cox harped on about the war in here the other night, plenty of blood-and-guts stuff. I don't know what she thinks she's proving by lying, except that maybe she's worried about him too."

"But Paul said whoever did this must keep up. Did you find any other record of Nate Cox visiting the rifle range?"

119

"Nothing. Same thing you found. I went back two years and Cox was only there once, the day after Newby was killed, if you don't worry about all the ripped and torn pages. They kept reminding me that the log was not a necessary or legal record. I'm tracking down the others who were there that same day, but so far no one remembers him at all." Willy looked cranky. He had completely ignored his beer all night. Suddenly he pushed away his full mug and stood up. "I don't know what the hell the connection is, but I'll find it. Tomorrow. The day after. Right now I'm going home."

Pete was so tired that once he got home he went straight to bed. But as was the case more often of late, once he hit the cold sheets he lay there shivering and thinking, watching his life flash before his eyes in painful review.

Finally the ghosts brought Pete kicking and screaming to that very day, rewinding and replaying everything Glen Newcomb had said, and in reviewing their conversation Pete finally had to admit that he might have been wrong in several of his previous assumptions. For one thing, he should have known Connie was too honest for any prolonged sneaking around, and for another, it seemed he was wrong in assuming that Glen and Connie were still in touch in any significant way. "She left me," Glen had said, and thinking of those words for the hundredth time it finally sank in to Pete's woodlike brain that whatever had happened between Connie and Glen, she *had* left him, and she had come back here, alone.

Suddenly Pete was sick of it all, sick of the awkward meetings and thirdhand conversations and his own inaction and self-pity and jealous rage. He sat up and grabbed the phone.

"Hello," she said into the phone, sounding wide awake and on edge.

"It's Pete."

120

There was a silence on the other end of the phone that lasted long enough for Pete to read things into it and then to read them right out of it again.

"Hi."

Pete stood up and started to walk around his bed as far as the phone cord would take him. Then he turned and walked back. "Listen, I want to . . ." What did he want? He wanted to see her. He wanted to talk to her. Why couldn't he just say that?

"Listen, what are you doing Monday night?" He meant to go on to say other things but the minute the words were out he realized that that was all the action that was needed. Connie would understand. She would see that those words, coming from him, were monumental enough alone.

"I have to go to the school Christmas party. Obligatory. Pain of death. You want to come along?"

Pete coughed to cover his surprise. "Sure," he said. And then just in case she remembered how unsure his "sure" had sometimes been, he added, "Yes. Yes, I'd like to."

"I warn you. You'll be bored. I'd better drive so you can't escape. I'll pick you up at eight." She hung up the phone so fast that for a minute Pete thought he had dreamt it. He stared at the phone for a long time and only truly believed he had really made the call when he realized his palms were wet.

The school Christmas party.

It wasn't much, but it was a start.

Chapter
14

At first Pete couldn't understand what was the matter with Rita. After two sleepless nights full of ghosts of Christmas futures he had walked down the hall Monday morning tapping out "Jingle Bells" on the walls only to find Andy just disappearing through the door and Rita mopping up coffee, gritting her teeth.

"Get him out of here! I tell you, if you don't get him out of here I'm going to do something drastic. I'm going to . . . I'm going to . . ."

Rita's definition of *drastic* was usually something along the lines of a good stiff frown, but just then the phone rang. When it turned out to be Maxine calling from Bradford when she was supposed to be in school, Pete decided to take Andy to the barn for the day anyway, just in case. Besides, Andy would help him to keep his own thoughts on his job instead of on the evening with Connie that loomed ahead.

Pete was going to a party with Connie. Every time he remembered that fact he stopped moving and stared down at his feet in surprise until someone prodded him from behind. Andy was a good prodder. He prodded

Pete into the truck, and then somehow he prodded Pete and the truck toward Jerry's barn.

"Whew!" said Andy, once they were under way. "Am I glad to get out of there today. I tell you, everybody's nuttier than Mrs. Potts, and I don't know who's worse, Rita or Allison. All I did was say, 'Merry Christmas' and spill a little coffee. Cripes. And I tried to see if Allison wanted to go to Bradford tonight and shop around—you know, check out the lights and stuff. There's only nine days till Christmas! You know what she said? She said she was a little too old for me! I said, 'Aw, come on, be a sport,' and she said wasn't I afraid she'd shoot me? What's the matter with everybody, anyway?"

"Yup," said Pete, who wasn't listening.

They weren't using any power tools today, which was lucky for Pete's wandering mind as well as for Andy's feet and fingers. When Paul Roose pulled into the yard in the squad car Pete felt fairly safe in leaving Andy with a hammer and nails and following Paul Roose into the white pine forest.

"What are you doing?"

Paul stood in the middle of the forest and looked around. "Trying to figure the best shot. What do you think?"

Pete thought that Paul must be AWOL from the police desk, but he didn't much care. It was just the kind of forced mental occupation that Pete needed. He looked around him. Trees. "I'd say he'd have to get out of the trees. There isn't much of a clear shot at the barn from in here."

Paul Roose nodded. "So how do you get out of the trees?"

"Go higher up."

Paul Roose dipped his head at Pete as a taciturn

teacher might at his star pupil. "High ground. Let's go."

Pete trailed through the whispering pines behind Paul as he followed the rise of the land, seemingly on some private track that only Paul could see. The spongy earth rose steadily under Pete's feet and the trees began to thin. Then Paul stopped.

"What do you see?"

Pete gazed ahead, and there, almost level with his newfound position, was Pease Street. He turned around, and there, clearly visible, was the roof of Jerry's barn at a distance that Pete would have judged to be about one hundred yards. He looked at Paul, and Paul's grim mouth twitched at one corner.

"What do you figure?"

"Someone driving down Pease Street saw Jerry on the barn and decided to take a potshot at him for the hell of it."

"Think so? Got an hour?"

"Me? I guess so."

"Come on."

Paul set off, down the rise this time. Pete felt just as he used to as a child when his father was trying to teach him something. Show, don't tell. Back at the barn he spoke to Andy and nervously handed him the truck keys in case he wasn't back by lunch. He climbed into the squad car beside Paul and set off—this time, Pete was somehow not surprised to discover, to Sarah Abrew's street.

Sarah Abrew lived in the more congested area of the island off Main Street, but still, most of Sarah's street was thickly fringed with scrub pines and bull briars. Paul Roose drove beyond Sarah's house to the end of the dead-end street, pulled the squad car into the trees as far as he could comfortably go, and got out. He walked

Pete back to the road, turned around, and faced the woods.

"Well?"

The car was barely visible, and at night would have been invisible.

"Let's go." He entered the bull briars with what, for Paul, came as close to cheer as Paul seemed to get.

Pete snapped up his jacket and plunged in after him.

"What did we learn that night at Sarah's?" Paul asked.

"Trajectory," Pete answered, starting to get a little more enthusiastic about this game. "You figured it was a downward-slanting shot from about a hundred yards, right?"

Paul plunged forward, again following the rise in the land. He broke free of the dry black branches into a clearing, and Pete followed and stopped, staring. Of course!

Ahead of him the old stone Indian tower loomed out of the forest. He turned around and saw what he had seen in the past and had not until now remembered— the old-fashioned brick-colored shingles of Sarah's tiny roof.

Paul watched Pete as he looked around.

"You'd see the lit window at night," said Pete. "A clear shot. But *why?*"

Paul shrugged and about-faced for the woods again. Pete raked a few brambles out of his hair and plunged after him, his mind racing. Who was this who was seeking out his targets this way? And why these targets? Had he known Newby would be at Sarah's? Had he suspected Jerry would be on his roof?

This time the squad car cruised straight down Main Street and parked across the street from Beston's Store. "And you know all about this one. You saw the muzzle flash and ran straight for it up the hill, the high ground, the clear spot, the sure bet.''

He pulled out and turned left on Shore Road, this time cutting behind the center of town onto the dirt road that skirted the hill behind Main Street. The hill would have given the sniper a good clean view of Evelyn Waxman perched on the steps of Beston's Store.

But *why?*

Of course the sniper would know that Evelyn would be there—everyone knew that Evelyn would be there leading the sing. And she was the main voice protesting the condos. *Was* it Nate who did this? Pete could only consider Allison's lies and edgy behavior as proof of her own concerns and therefore as another nail in her father's coffin. But what if it wasn't Nate? Pete felt even more nervous at that thought and took a minute to analyze it. True, Ozzie was a son of a bitch, and hold-a-grudge Pease wasn't any day at the beach, but still, they were Nashtoba's own sons of bitches and grudge holders. Nate Cox, on the other hand, was fairly new to the island, and even though Pete worked with Allison, he knew her very little, after all. Wouldn't he prefer it to be this relative newcomer rather than someone he had grown up around, someone he had known all his life?

But although these roads were well known on the island, they weren't roads that the average person would use to get from here to there. Would Nate Cox be apt to travel them? Pete doubted it. Ozzie, on the other hand, just might. From these elevated viewpoints he could see Close Harbor as well as the Sound, and he could cast his weather eye over his salt-water domain. Cyrus Pease would be less apt to travel around on a sea weather watch, but still, he was a farmer who knew the land, who knew the meanings and uses of its rises and dips.

Paul Roose dropped Pete off at the barn. As Pete slid

out of the cruiser Betsy Beggs came out of the house and met Pete between the barn and her car. "Jerry's coming home in the morning," she said. "I'm off to get his Christmas present while he's not around. I'm looking for a new armchair, one with that leather upholstery he likes. Do you think you could hide it at your house?"

"Sure," said Pete, trying to visualize one square foot of open space in his house while at the same time trying not to think about all the Christmas presents he had yet to buy, some of which would have to be mailed. Or *all* of which would have to be mailed. What was he going to do? Florida? Maine? Here? He thought again about Connie and the night's plans. There was no need, he decided, to make up his mind just yet. And there was also no need to buy presents until he knew which people he would be able to deliver to in person.

He pushed Christmas into the back of his mind once again, and it managed to remain there for a half hour or so, or at least until Andy started whistling "Joy to the World." It wasn't the easiest song to whistle, even if you weren't tone deaf, which Andy was. If Pete had to listen to amateurs sing Christmas carols he'd rather hear somebody who sounded like a cross between Ethel Merman and Janis Joplin, the way Connie did. He smiled to himself and started to whistle along with Andy. Then he thought about seeing Connie that very night and the tune faded from his lips before the cold clutch of fear.

The evening presented a lot of problems for Pete, but clothes was not one of them. He owned one Harris tweed jacket and one respectable pair of pants; he ironed up his best all-cotton white shirt and laid out his one muted simple tie beside it. It wasn't exactly understated elegance, but it was understated, all right, and Pete figured it would do. He showered and shaved for the second time that day, and in a wild moment splashed on a little after-shave that Maxine had given him last year for Christmas. He got dressed, ran a comb through his wet hair, and sat down at his kitchen table to wait.

And to think. Connie didn't usually last too long as a party person—she was more of an intense flash that came on strong and burned out quickly. Pete didn't expect they'd be at the school too long, and there would probably be plenty of time at the end of the evening for that much-needed talk.

That, of course, was the problem.

What did he want to say? Or perhaps more important, what did he want to hear?

He heard her car. He heard the front door open without a knock the way it was opened by anyone who knew him. He heard high heels click across the pine floors and he heard a soft tap on the kitchen door. He pulled it open, opened his mouth to speak, and left it hanging there.

Her long coat was draped over her shoulders, her dress was a plain one that became disconcertingly unplain the minute she moved, and her hair was twisted up in back and sparkling with a fine mist. Her heels brought her close to eye level, and she looked him up and down with a decisive appreciation that at once seemed to take the questions right out of the night.

"Thank God you're not in a Santa suit or wearing a musical tie."

"Do you want me to drive?"

She looked down at her legs, and Pete looked with her. "I haven't yet had a pair of nylons that's survived a ride in your truck. *I'll* drive. My tires are bald. If this rain turns to snow, we'll be spending the night in a drift." She spun on her heels and led them back down the hall.

Pete clambered into her tiny car with "Let It Snow,

Let It Snow, Let It Snow" running merrily through his head.

Even the artificial Christmas tree in the school lobby looked nice. As Pete and Connie walked into the room side by side he could feel the eyes of others in their wake. Pete knew almost everyone at the party. The municipal sector was represented by the police chief and Ted and Ernie Ball. Besides all of Connie's co-teachers and Pete's old school principal, Mrs. Smoot, he saw Jerry and Betsy Beggs, and although Pete couldn't see him over the crowd, he knew Bert Barker was there because his was the first individual voice to pierce through the babble.

"It's people like the Waxmans that really crack me up. They move onto the island and try to burn the bridge right after them. What if we burned that bridge before they got here, huh?"

"Oh, I don't know," said Ernie Ball. "I think people like the Waxmans have contributed a lot to this place. It's not the days it once was around here, Bert. You have to start looking to the future. Some of us have been stuck here in the trees so long we can't see the forest, you know what I mean? It's up to people like the Waxmans to see this place for what it is, for what's different about it, to try to keep it from turning into someplace just like everyplace else. I'm not against *some* expansion—it just oughta fit in, that's all."

"Fit in!" said Jean Martell. "But who says what fits in? What about my constitutional rights? What if I like condos, Ernie?"

"I think that in addition to retaining the local flavor of the place, the finite nature of the resources of the island has to be taken into consideration," said Mrs. Smoot. "Two hundred condominium units perched on the fragile shore . . ."

"Finite!" snorted Bert. "What's *finite* mean when it's a real word, heh?"

Pete and Connie exchanged glances and gazed off toward the window where the police chief stood alone. A long table covered with a white cloth lined the window bay and several of the guests were delving into the reindeer cookies and the inevitable red punch. He and Connie moved away from the crowd toward the chief, but soon others circled around with cookie crumbs on their clothes and insinuating smiles on their faces, and Pete and Connie were no longer alone.

Yet as the night wore on something happened. An old, nonverbal communication that had once thrived between them began to come back to life, isolating them from the other people in the room even as they mingled side by side among them, drawing them closer and closer, and finally distracting them sufficiently so that neither of them seemed to hear anyone else correctly or to be able to respond to them just right. By ten o'clock Pete decided they'd been there long enough. He leaned across the punch bowl until his mouth was near her ear. "Hey," he said. "Let's—"

The glass punch bowl shattered into a million pieces, and red punch flooded everything in sight.

Pete stared at Connie. A wet, soggy splotch darkened the front of her wool dress and her usually rosy cheeks were greenish white. "She's hit!" he hollered, and grabbed her, expecting her to tumble to the ground, but Connie just stared at Pete, her knees rigid, her eyes full of terror. The chief elbowed his way up and tried to ease Connie down, but it soon turned into a wrestling match, Connie clutching at Pete to keep her feet under her, the chief trying to settle her to the ground.

Finally Connie hollered.

"Punch! It's punch! I'm all right, you goddamned elephant—get off me!"

The circle backed up. Connie struggled to her feet alone. "Jesus Christ! I'm *all right.*" She swatted away the chief's hands. "I wasn't hit, all right?"

And neither was anyone else.

'Everyone just stay put," barked the chief. "Ernie, you're in charge in here. Nobody leaves." He grabbed Ted Ball and headed for the door.

"Wait here," Pete said to Connie, and he charged after the police.

"Oh, no you don't!" Connie charged out after him. Outside, the chief and Ernie had stopped. Across the road a lone figure stood staking out the high ground, a soft hill across Shore Road in the middle of a tangle of deadened beach plum bushes.

The chief drew his gun. From the top of the hill, Paul Roose hollered. "Chief!" He held something up. The chief and Ernie and Pete and Connie scrambled across the road and up the hill to Paul.

"Another cartridge casing. Some broken branches. I figure he tore off that way."

"You two get out of here," the chief said to Pete and Connie. Pete's first impulse was to argue, but somewhere along the line Connie had moved up against him, and suddenly he was more aware of the pressure of her body than he was of a potential sniper in the scrub.

They returned together to her car.

Chapter 15

Connie always agonized after the fact over the right and wrong decisions in her life, but at the actual moment of crisis her brain was the first thing to go. Usually it was disastrous. This time it was just right. She pulled up outside Factotum and, without thinking at all, got out of the car and followed Pete in.

True, they were arguing at the time.

"It wasn't just the punch," said Pete. "Your face was this terrible color. You looked terrified."

"I *was* terrified, goddamnit! You were standing right in front of the punch bowl when it got blown to smithereens. Right in the window! I thought *you* got hit! Your whole crotch was oozing all this—"

"Punch," said Pete, looking down at himself for the first time. "See? I told you it looked like blood."

"And then you go running *outside*, right across the road and into the bushes in case he wanted another shot!"

"I learned something about the sniper today." Pete walked down the hall toward the kitchen. "He searches out high ground. There was the perfect rise right across

132

the road. I thought we were going to catch him this time."

Connie snorted in exasperation. "The only one who's going to get caught is the next one in the line of fire."

Pete threw his jacket on the kitchen table, untied his tie, and rolled up his sleeves. "It'll be all right. You want a beer?" He turned toward the refrigerator.

"All right," repeated Connie bitterly, but Pete must have thought she meant about the drink. He turned back to her with a Ballantine and only stopped as he caught her eye. What had he seen there that had stopped him that way? She didn't know. She only knew that what she had seen in his made her feel like . . . like what? Like an ancient family heirloom, something old and treasured and valued that could never be replaced.

Connie never knew what happened to the beer. The feel of him was like the first hot rays of sun at the end of a long, cold, wet Nashtoba winter.

Connie woke early but slowly the next morning, assimilating things one step at a time. The first thing she thought was that it had been a long time since she had slept so soundly. The second thing she thought was that she felt unusually warm and dry and cozy in her drafty apartment and lumpy bed. The third thing she thought was that she was feeling pretty special this morning—sort of contented and, well, cherished. Then she realized that there was actually something warm and cozy nestled up against her whole back side and her eyes slammed open and she saw Pete's room that had once been her room too and just like that she was wide awake.

He must have felt her body come to life because his arm tightened around her. "Don't go."

Connie rolled over and raised herself up on one

elbow. "Have you given any thought to the fact that it's risky hanging around you? Too many bullets nearby. First there you are outside the window at Sarah's with a bullet whizzing over your head, then you're way in back at the carols when he pops off again, and it could well have been you on Jerry's roof. And last night—"

Pete flipped onto his back, groaned and opened his eyes. "Is that all you can say this morning? Aren't you supposed to—"

"I'm serious, damn you. What if this crazy sniper *is* after you? You know what I think? I think you should go to Florida or Maine or wherever you plan to go for Christmas right now. Today. Get out of here."

"And here I was thinking of sticking around." He looked at her with those deep, dark eyes that nowadays always seemed to be demanding something of her, and suddenly Connie felt like a crook out on parole or a player in a monopoly game with Pete in the role of banker. She could say the right things, do the right things, and she would advance to Go and collect her two hundred dollars. She could blow it and end up in jail.

All this analyzing was wearing her out. She got up and disappeared into the bathroom before Pete could see her face. When she came back out she changed the subject—sort of.

"I still think somebody's trying to shoot you. And who was he trying to shoot at that party if it wasn't you? Jerry Beggs? Was he trying a second time for Jerry—is that what you think?"

Pete folded his hands behind his head and frowned at the ceiling. "Jerry. Maybe. I don't know. Something's all wrong about this."

Connie snorted. "Maybe he was after the punch all along."

"Yeah," said Pete, but not as if he really heard her.

Suddenly he rolled over and grabbed her by the leg. "Hey. We have to talk."

Connie wiggled out of his grip, her heart sinking. *Talk.* This could only mean digging up pasts, wrenching out explanations that were no explanations at all, facing The Great Stone Face of Pete's pain—pain *she* had caused him.

"Can't we eat first?" She sailed into the kitchen and began to construct two huge bowls of Wheaties and bananas.

After the Wheaties it seemed like a good idea to take their coffee cups back to bed to talk there, only they forgot to talk, of course. Then Connie had to scramble to make it to school.

Reprieve.

Pete stared bemusedly out of Sarah Abrew's living room window until the old lady rapped her braided rug with her cane.

"Hey! The selectmen. The selectmen advised *what* about the dump?"

Pete snapped his eyes back to the paper. "The selectmen. 'The selectmen advised . . .' " Where was he? It was no use. He folded the paper, threw it down, and got up to stand by the window. "You can hardly see the Indian Tower from here, can you?"

"I can hardly see, period. Now the school. You say nobody was hurt at the school?"

Pete turned back to face her. "Just the punch. No great loss. And my only good pair of pants—also no great loss." Then he remembered Connie's dress. That *would* be a bit of a loss! But he didn't tell Sarah about Connie's dress, afraid that she'd hear the wonder in his voice at the mention of Connie and he wasn't ready to share Connie with anyone else just yet. "When do you leave for Baltimore?"

"Monday. And you promised me you'd pick up the beach plum jelly and the sherry. Did you forget? Eight days till Christmas, you know."

Pete jumped up. "Of course not. I'll do it now. I have some Christmas shopping of my own to do."

He leaned over her and kissed her, as he always did, and Sarah squeezed his hand, as she always did. "You did say nobody was hurt?"

"Nobody. Willy and Paul took off into the woods after the sniper, but I haven't seen them yet. I don't know if they found out anything. I'll let you know what I hear."

"You tell that young man to do something before this sniper ruins Christmas."

"It's ruined already," he said, but he spoke as if from an old record, and after he spoke he realized that he wasn't so sure he really meant that anymore. Still, he was surprised at the vehemence of Sarah's reaction.

"I am so sick of that word, *ruined!* I am sick to death of everyone getting so all-fired down in the mouth over Christmas! What it *means!* What it *costs!* When it starts, when it ends! Just take what you want out of it, spend what you want to spend on it, make it mean what you want it to mean. Stop *moaning* about it!"

Pete kneeled down in front of her chair. "But make it mean *what*, Sarah? Nowadays what *does* all this mean?"

Sarah appeared to give that some thought. "I guess I'd say Christmas means another chance. Maybe that's why I like it. I'm eighty-six years old. I don't have too many chances left. And yet every year Christmas comes around again, reminding me there's one more go in the old girl yet." She shook her head. "I keep thinking this year I'll do that one thing I loused up last time around. Yes, I guess that must be it. Another chance." She leaned forward and grasped his chin in her hands. "But to *have* another chance you have to *take* another chance."

Pete looked at Sarah and was suddenly frightened by what she meant to him, by what a lot of people meant to him, and by how little time he might have to let them know it. But after all, how much time did he need? He reached out and held on to Sarah's hand.

"I love you, Sarah."

"Oh, I love you too," she said, but she said it with the impatience of an old woman who didn't want to waste time on things they both already knew. "Now who cares what Christmas means? It's something to do. It's got good songs. It's *nice*. Stop worrying about it so much and enjoy it, will you?"

Pete kissed Sarah again. As he left he whistled "Good King Wenceslas," Sarah's favorite Christmas song.

Chapter 16

"Seven shopping days till Christmas!" blared the radio, and Pete, now that he had finally decided to start, began to panic. His parents, Polly, Sarah, Rita, Maxine, Andy, Allison, Connie? Yes, Connie. Another chance. He wanted to get something special for Connie. He remembered the claw-foot bathtub he'd planned to give Connie before she left. He could give her the tub. No, he couldn't give her the tub. She had no place to put it. It was too personal. Not the tub. Not this year. Another chance. But what if . . . No, not the tub.

He wandered into the Jam and Jelly Shop and stumbled around blindly, his mind on the night before. *To have another chance you have to take another chance.* Why hadn't he pinned her down this morning? Why hadn't he insisted she stay and talk? Why hadn't he insisted they make plans to meet again? He would find her today. He'd *act.*

"Help you, Pete?"

Pete's head snapped up. "Hi, May. Sarah's jelly. I forget what—"

May Simms pulled a box of assorted jams and jellies

off the table and plunked it down by the register. "She always takes this—the beach plum, apple butter, rose hip box. Folks coming up soon?"

"No." It suddenly dawned on Pete that for the first time in his life he might not see his parents on Christmas. Was he going to miss them? Yes, he was. Very much. Would they miss Christmas on Nashtoba? He thought so. Yes! That's what he'd get his parents—a variety pack of Christmas on Nashtoba, starting right here with the jams and jellies and going on to coffee beans and mulled cider mix from Beston's Store, and . . . If he mailed things to Florida would they get there in time? He'd make sure of it. Overnight express, or one of those things. *If* he stayed here, that was. What if Connie didn't stay? Where would he go? But he'd have to mail it now whether he went to Florida or not. Yes, that's what he'd do—he'd mail it now.

He bought Sarah's jelly and a mix of things for his parents.

He left the center of town, resisted turning left on Shore Road toward Pease Street, and decided to swing by the Keileys', who had been calling Factotum for several days, wanting their outside water shut off.

Art Keiley had other things on his mind besides water. "Old military weapon, I hear, Pete? This sniper is using an old military weapon?"

"That's the best guess."

"Come here." He waved Pete inside and up his polished staircase to the second floor. In the papered wall of the extra bedroom upstairs was a small door. Art Keiley pushed it open, ducked under the eaves, and disappeared inside. Pete followed.

"Here." Art straightened up from on old leather-strapped trunk and turned on Pete and for one second Pete felt a flush of fear. Art Keiley was a relative newcomer to Nashtoba. Pete didn't know Art from a hole in the wall, so to speak. He was World War II vintage. He was two feet from Pete. With a gun in his hand.

"German Luger. Nifty little side arm, wouldn't you say? Ever seen one of these?"

Pete shook his head and wiped his brow. "Does it work?"

"You bet it does." He fondled the cold metal lovingly. "Nabbed this off a dead German on Omaha Beach."

"What kind of bullets?"

"Nine-millimeter."

Nine-millimeter—the same as Jack Whiteaker's find, the same as the police use.

"Are you supposed to have that, Art?"

Art shook his head, tucking the gun back in its hiding place regretfully. "Just a little souvenir. No harm in it."

Not until it kills somebody, thought Pete.

Back outside Art leaned against a tree and told Pete how busy he was now that he was retired, while Pete drained off the water.

Pete left Keiley's for Jerry's barn and forced himself to stay there until it was almost dark. Only then did he drive to Pease Street.

Connie wasn't home.

The phone was ringing as he opened his front door, and making some illogical assumptions as to who it might be, he raced up to Rita's desk and snatched at the phone.

"Hello!"

"Finally," said a voice that contained a fair amount of crust.

"Hello," Pete repeated idiotically, unable to place it.

"Cyrus here. Cyrus Pease. I wonder if you might be able to stop by. The farm, I mean. Got something to show you."

140

"I thought you were in Florida."

"Sister's. Boston. Came all the way back when Glen told me about this weapon being military. Are you coming or not?"

"If this is a police matter maybe I should get hold of the chief."

"Leave that fool chief out of it. At least till you hear this. Are you coming or not? I don't want to hang around all December waiting for you to show."

Pete started to feel a little dumb. "I'm on my way," he said.

Cyrus Pease's farm was gloomy and poorly lit. Pete picked his way over soggy ground to the front door of the farmhouse and knocked. After some moments an additional light flicked on behind the curtained window and the door opened.

"Get on in," said Cyrus. He appeared to be alone. Pete followed him down the same dim hall he had followed Glen Newcomb down a few days ago, into the same room full of guns. Cyrus ignored the shelves and cases of guns and went instead for the phone on the desk—or, more accurately, for the black box beside it. He pressed the button on the answering machine. "Listen."

Pete listened. It sounded to Pete like Cyrus had rewound his entire answering machine tape and was now playing back the string of messages. Cyrus stopped the tape.

"Well? Hear that?"

Pete didn't know what he was supposed to be hearing, and consequently assumed that he hadn't heard it. "No," he said. The half-lit room with shadows of guns on every wall was giving him the creeps.

Cyrus shot him a disgruntled look and pressed the button to rewind the tape again. "This first voice. I want to know if you know who it is."

141

Alerted now, Pete listened closely to the first message. The beginning of it appeared to have been partially taped over.

". . . won't be moving yet, not till I sell," the unknown voice began in the middle. "I'm home most days. It's in good shape. Give me a call if you're interested."

Pete shook his head. The voice was male, sounded neither young nor old, and was not particularly distinctive, but Pete was almost sure he'd heard the voice recently, or at least one like it. "I don't know. What about it?"

"Some fellow left this message on my machine a while back, wanting to sell me an M-1 Garand. I already had Buck's—I didn't want it. I didn't return the call."

"Who was it?"

Cyrus grunted. "If I knew would I be asking you? He didn't leave his name—just a Nashtoba number. I remember the exchange. Don't recall the number. That's all."

"Do you remember the rest of the message?"

"Just did I want a Garand in good condition, and that if I did to call that number—he'd be around till he sold it—call during the day. Something like that."

"Play it again, Cyrus."

Cyrus played it again. It didn't help.

"Do you remember *when* the call came?"

Cyrus pushed the button on the machine and let it play longer this time, through four or five more messages, before he stopped it. "That message there, the one from the fellow named Bradley—he's an old buddy of mine from the war. I know that came in on December seventh. He calls me every year on Pearl Harbor Day. So this mystery message here—this came before that."

"How long before that?"

"A while before. Not too long before. There's four

or five messages in between. I don't get a message every day."

December seventh. Pearl Harbor Day. The day Newby was shot.

Pete stood up. "The chief has to know about this, Cyrus."

Cyrus shrugged. "Reckon so. Didn't want to tear off over there without knowing who it was. You get around a lot, know most everybody—thought maybe you'd recognize it."

That remark set Pete off on an interesting line of thought. Whoever made this call made it from Nashtoba. It was most likely from someone Pete and Cyrus knew. Cyrus hadn't wanted to hand the tape over to the chief until he knew who it was he was handing over. It was thinking Pete could understand, to a point.

"Here." Cyrus unplugged the machine, wrapped the cord around it, and handed it to Pete.

"Why don't you take it? He's going to want to talk to you anyway."

Cyrus shook his head. "You take it. He's your big buddy. He knows where I am if he wants to talk, but I don't know any more'n I told you."

"But you'll probably have to make a—"

"You should take it in yourself, Cy," said a voice from the door, and Pete turned around to see Glen Newcomb framed there in the faint light. "I'll go with you if you like."

"I'll do this my way. Let that fancy cop use his own gas and come out here if he wants. I'll be staying here two more days—that'll give him time enough."

Glen Newcomb stepped through the doorway and up to Pete. "I'll do it," he said, and he held out his hand for the machine.

It must have been the poor light, or all those guns, or the length of Glen's shadow on the wall. Pete hung tight to the answering machine and circled around Glen, heading for the door. "No, thanks—I can handle it."

Glen followed him. "A minute, please. I believe I have a word or two to—"

"Glen!" his uncle called from behind him.

Glen stopped. "A minute, Cy."

Pete kept moving.

"Pete knows the way out. Help me with this box."

After another second's hesitation Glen retreated toward the gun room, and Pete hurried out.

They sat at the kitchen table in the chief's house and listened again to the tape.

"Is there any way to retrieve the missing portion under the other message?" asked Pete.

"I don't know but I'll sure find out. Tell me what he thought it said again?"

Pete told him again. "He'll talk to you—he just didn't want to do it now, I guess."

"You're damned right he'll talk to me." It was a tough-cop line, conjuring up rubber truncheons and bread and water, and Willy looked a little embarrassed after he'd said it.

"Glen Newcomb was there. Or at least he showed up near the end."

The chief looked up.

"He offered to bring this in to you, but I thought I'd better. So what about last night? Did you and Paul find anything?"

The chief shook his head, but said nothing.

"How about the casing—was it a match?"

The chief nodded yes, but still didn't comment further. Pete tried again.

"How about Nate Cox? Where was he last night?"

"Home alone," said the chief, but not as if it mattered.

"And Ozzie too?"

Another nod.

"And Cyrus is back. Alone. I guess that's the trouble with this whole thing—that most of the snipings occur at an hour when most sensible people are home alone anyway. Or with a loved one who could be expected to lie if they weren't. But you didn't find anybody last night? Nothing today—no tracks, no threads, no fibers?"

Willy didn't answer that. Instead he said, "I'd like to find that weapon. I'm tracking down World War Two vets right now."

"Do you have Art Keiley on your vet list? He has a German Luger, some nine-millimeter thing."

Willy made a note on a greasy-looking piece of paper. "I don't expect these vets to come marching into the station with their weapons if they aren't supposed to have them. If you see any more lying around, let me know."

Pete nodded. "So where does this leave you?"

Willy crossed his arms over the answering machine and stared at it morosely. "Eating frozen turkey pie and a beer instead of crispy goose and Pinot Noir at my sister's in Connecticut."

Pete laid a hand on Willy's shoulder as he left. "Cheer up—you've got a week to go."

It was eleven o'clock when Pete left Willy's, but he drove by Connie's anyway. The Triumph was outside and at least one light was on, but Pete moved reluctantly by without stopping. He'd seen her too little today, but now it was definitely too late.

Chapter
17

"We go to Aunt Ethel's *every year*," said Rita. "I mean, I don't understand what her *problem* is! She loves it there. And now she tells me she wants to learn to ski and she needs these three-hundred-dollar *skis* for Christmas, and the *boots*, and the *poles* and the whole outfit, and that child has never been on skis in her life! *Honestly!* I've always wanted to learn to sail but I'm not going to go out and buy a *yacht!*"

Pete looked at the clock on Rita's desk. Six hours until the bell released Connie from school. He wanted to get Connie something symbolic this Christmas. He picked up the picture of Maxine that was over a year old. He usually gave Maxine something goofy for Christmas. Was it time to get her something very adult instead? He looked at Rita's shining black head and downy, buckled eyebrows. Conversely, he wanted to get Rita something fun.

"And *where* do you ski?" Rita went on. "Maine. Vermont. Three hundred miles away from home! Don't think I don't know what she's plotting, all right!"

On the other hand, thought Pete, maybe a set of boxing gloves would be a safer bet.

"And Polly called again. She wants to know where you're going. I told her all I knew was that you weren't coming to Aunt Ethel's. And don't forget to call your mother—I told her you would. Honestly, Pete, you have *got* to make up your mind! And I told Alton Martell you'd be over today without fail about the addition. Which works out fine since Betsy Beggs called and wants you to lay off the barn for a bit—she's afraid if you arrive Jerry won't rest like he's supposed to. And Mrs. Potts is calling again. And Allison's going to be late so someone has to pick up Irene Blakely and take her to her appointment at Hardy's. Now *where in the world* are you going to put Jerry's chair?"

Pete looked behind him at the stuffed leather armchair, wrapped in plastic, looming in the middle of what was once his living room's rug. "I don't know," he said. "Let's leave it there and decorate it." He turned around and grinned at Rita. Rita's mouth opened, but nothing came out.

Pete took advantage of the brief silence and headed out for Alton's, but only after he checked the clock again. Five hours and forty-five minutes to go. And seven days.

Martelli's restaurant looked cold and bleak so early in the morning with the chairs on top of the tables and the whitecaps in the harbor glinting through the glass. The un-Italian–looking Alton, red-haired and freckled and skinny as a toothpick, led Pete out into the bitter wind and sketched a large rectangle into the air off the right-hand flank of the building.

"Here. Mostly glass. It'll face northwest so it won't get too hot in the summer, and we'll close this part in the winter if it gets too cold. Lots of plants and glass-

147

topped tables with yellow metal chairs. Run it out about this far.'' Alton walked across the grass and stopped a considerable distance from the existing restaurant wall. "What do you figure?''

Pete figured Alton was counting on a lot of new business soon, that's what Pete figured. He looked out across the harbor, past the hotel, to Ozzie's little bait shop and the expanse of beach grass beyond. He squinted his eyes and tried to picture row after row of identical boxes with artsy modern angles, matching decks, and sliding glass. He then pictured an army of white shoes and white belts marching down the sand-covered road to Martelli's, seeing the glass and plants and bright light and asking for a seat in the sunroom, please.

"Well? What do you figure? Always been kind of a dream of mine, this room.''

Pete tried to figure whether someone would kill for this dream. He looked again at the square of grass Alton had marked out. Connie had always said it was better to be a doer than a dreamer. You dream, you get disappointed. You do, you get it done. So what if your definition of *to do* is to kill?

"I couldn't start till spring,'' said Pete. "You'd be in a rush for summer. And that's assuming nobody shoots me first.''

Alton followed Pete's gaze out across the harbor toward Ozzie's shop. "From what Jean says things are going nowhere slow down at the station. First Ted does something, then Paul does it over, then the chief does it over twice.''

"Do you shoot, Alton?''

Alton grinned. "I hope so. Dunno yet. Take a look at this.'' He turned his back on the wind, led them inside, and crossed the dining room to the office at the back. "Andy's been doing a good job on the furniture,'' he said, rubbing a hand over the newly refinished desk. He leaned down behind it and surfaced with a shotgun. "In case we get robbed. Haven't used it yet—hope I never do."

Pete stared at the ugly double barrels. "You've got a license for that?"

"Of course I do. With my wife working at the station? You think I'm nuts?"

Pete considered. You'd have to be nuts to kill a whole string of people in the hopes of financial gain from a development project. You'd have to sell a lot of fettucini Alfredo to make something like that worthwhile. Looking at it in that light, it again seemed to Pete that the chief's whole premise about the condos was somehow out of whack. People didn't *do* these things! He settled a few preliminary details with Alton and left, driving past the Whiteaker Hotel and the bait shop as he went. DILLINGHAM BAIT AND TACKLE. BOATS TO RENT. CHARTER FISHING. CRAWLERS, SEA WORMS, SQUID, SAND EELS, SHINERS. Suddenly Pete grinned. He knew what he was going to get for Rita, at least. He swung the truck around and pulled up behind the shop.

The smell of old fish was especially strong today. Or was it the smell of old bodies? Ozzie himself didn't seem to be swaddled in the spirit of the season. From ten feet outside the door Pete could hear him hollering away.

"I'll tell you when I feel like telling you, you old buzzard!"

A voice of considerably lower decibels rumbled back inaudibly. Pete hesitated with his hand on the door and suddenly felt it burst inward out of his grip.

"And don't call me, I'll call you!" Ozzie briskly ushered his first guest, Nate Cox, out the door and glared at his second one. "What do *you* want—first pick of the condos?"

Even in such a context Nate Cox's sullen eyes flickered at the mention of condos, but he didn't speak to Pete as he hastened past.

"No thanks—I'm Christmas shopping."

Ozzie about-faced and clumped in heavy boots across the bait shop's rickety floor. "What do you want? I don't have all day."

Why not? Pete wondered. "I want a boat. Sort of. I want to rent a sailboat for Rita next summer, teach her to sail. Can you make up a gift certificate for something like that?"

Ozzie stopped fussing around with a pile of tide charts and turned around to stare at Pete. "Optimistic, aren't you?"

"What do you mean?"

"You figure I'm not selling out?"

"I figure I'll get my money back all right if you do. Are you?"

"You want a Hobie Cat, a Sunfish, an hour, a day, a week—what?" Ozzie rattled off the various prices. "Tourist rates."

"What's your rate for locals?"

"You rent a sailboat, you're a tourist."

Pete glared at him. Ozzie glared back. Pete opted for the Hobie Cat and wrote out a check for rental of the boat for one day. Ozzie scribbled out "Good for one Hobie for one day" on the back of a tide chart and signed it.

As Pete reached the door of the shop Ozzie called after him, "Did you have a swell time at the school?"

Pete turned around, considering whether maybe it was just Ozzie, and not the bait, that smelled. "We would have, but they ran out of punch. Did you have a swell time in the war?"

"Leyte, Mindoro, Luzon, Okinawa, and caught in a typhoon. Swell!"

Pete pushed open the door.

"You don't get your money back if I'm in jail!" Ozzie shouted as he walked through it.

Pete decided to wipe the taste of Ozzie out of his mouth with a good dose of Christmas. He swung into town, parked the truck, and walked down Main Street, peering into shop windows as he went. He stopped in front of the jewelry store. A pair of earrings in the window caught his eye—showers of tiny gold stars suspended on threadlike gold chain. The earrings were adult enough and Christmasy enough to be just the thing for Maxine. He bought them.

Back at Factotum Rita was just hanging up the phone, frowning, and that meant maybe it was Connie who had called.

"That was Allison. She's not coming in at all. She said her father's sick."

"Anything serious?"

"She wouldn't say. You know Allison."

"Maybe I should stop over there."

Rita jumped up. "No. I'll send Andy."

But for once Pete argued her down. "No. Allison is my employee. It's my responsibility, not Andy's."

"You have to call your mother."

Pete stared at Rita. Why was she acting so strangely? He could call his mother anytime. "I'll run by Cox's first. I'll call when I get back."

Rita knotted up her eyebrows in that way that meant she was trying hard to think of another excuse to shoot at him. Pete left before she could do so.

Nate Cox's real estate office was empty, but the bell over its door jangled as he went in and Allison soon appeared through a door at the back. At the sight of Pete her skin turned so pink that it showed through the white-blond hair on her scalp.

151

"Rita says your father's sick. Anything serious? Need any help?"

She shook her head. She wasn't much with words, but she sure was good at staring. She was also getting pretty good at looking hurt.

"Listen, I know you think everyone around here hates your father's guts, but it's not true. Plenty of people are hoping that the condo deal goes through."

Allison continued to stare. And to wait. For what?

"I mean it, Allison. If your father's seriously sick—"

"He's not sick."

Pete turned away and roamed over to the desk that was centered on the right-hand half of the little room. On the desk was a Rolodex with a handful of cards, an appointment calendar that didn't seem to have anything on it, and a phone that wasn't ringing. Pete turned back to Allison. "Why did you say your father spent the war behind a desk?"

"Because he did."

"Your father told some stories that didn't happen behind any desk."

Allison said nothing.

"Listen, Allison—you're only making it worse for him if you lie."

Still she didn't speak, but the gray eyes didn't waver. Pete waved a hand around the room. "How's business?"

"All right."

"And your dad's not sick."

"No."

Pete gave up. "So let me know if you feel like coming back." He left the office feeling more uncomfortable around Allison by the minute and unable to put his finger on just why.

Two hours to go.

Pete returned to Factotum, retired to his kitchen and

ate lunch, then reached for his old-fashioned black rotary phone and called his mother.

"Are you coming?" his mother asked right off the bat.

"I don't know," Pete answered. "This sniper business is shaking things up. I hate to leave with—"

"Then we'll come up there," said his mother. "I mean we aren't *that* old! We could get there on—"

"No!" said Pete, panicked. He now had his heart set on *two* stockings on his fireplace, not a crowd of four. "I mean, I don't think you should. I don't think it's safe. There was another shooting just Monday and—"

"Then I think you should come right down here *now*," said his mother, sounding more than a little like Connie. It was a creepy thought.

"I can't leave now—I'm helping the chief."

"Ralph!" she hollered behind her. "He won't leave because of the sniper! Oh, Pete. I don't like the thought of you staying there alone. I think we should come up."

"No," said Pete fast. "This thing should wrap up soon and I'll be able to leave okay." Then Pete had an idea, a diversionary one. "Could I talk to Dad? I want to ask him something about the war."

"Ralph!" his mother hollered again, and disappeared. Somewhat to Pete's surprise, his father surfaced quickly on the other end of the phone.

"The war, you say, Pete?"

"Yeah, Dad. This sniper is using some old military ammunition and a military rifle. He's a pretty good shot. Did you use a rifle in the war?"

"M-1," said his father.

"Garand? Carbine?"

"Carbine."

"Were you any good?"

"We all had to qualify as marksmen, Pete."

"But could you shoot now? I mean, if you had to

153

could you hit something a hundred yards away? Is it like a bicycle, where once you learn you never fall off?"

His father chuckled. "Nobody said you never fell off, Pete. You never forget how to do it, but you don't necessarily have to be any good at it. No, I couldn't do very well today without a lot of practice, I don't think—not after all that time."

"Oh," said Pete. "Now an expert marksman, he'd be somewhat rare?"

"Well, your average Joes weren't necessarily such good shots, Pete. They drafted everybody. Even me." He chuckled again.

"But once you were in the service, did you shoot much?"

There was a minute's silence. "When they unloaded us onto some island and something rustled in the bushes we shot at it, Pete. Maybe I didn't know what was in there, but I knew what *could* have been in there. It was us or them, Pete."

"But did you—"

Suddenly Pete's father didn't seem to want to talk about it anymore. "Listen, why don't you get that sister of yours and come on down here. Why don't you do that? I don't think it's such a good idea you hanging around up there with a sniper on the loose."

"Well—"

"Here's your mother," said his father.

Pete's mother pushed on about Christmas until the phone felt like a pressure cooker against his ear. He started to watch the clock. When she finally hung up it was just about time for the last bell at school, if Pete's recollection served him right. He jumped up from the kitchen table and walked down the hall just in time to see Evan Spender leaning over Rita's desk, kissing her mouth. Pete retreated to his kitchen and stared at the kitchen clock some more. After all, the last bell was for

154

the students, not the teachers. Teachers had to stay after school and do things, didn't they? It wouldn't hurt to wait a while more—say, fifteen minutes.

Pete went back out, coughing a little this time, and Rita and Evan popped up from Jerry Beggs's chair.

"Oh! Pete. Evan and I wanted to run a quick errand. Could you watch the desk for half an hour?"

Pete looked at the clock, his heart sinking. "Sure."

"Maybe an hour?" added Evan.

Pete looked at the clock again. "Sure," he said, a little weaker this time.

"Actually," said Rita, "if it's going to be an hour, or maybe an hour and a half, it doesn't make much sense for me to come back at all, does it?"

"Not much sense," said Pete glumly, but Rita and Evan seemed to notice only the actual assent, not the tone associated with it. They left together.

A quick errand.

Right.

Pete sat down at the desk and stared at the clock.

Chapter
18

At four thirty the phone rang.

"Pete? Pete! I'm so glad this is you! You *must* come over right away. I think I've found the bullet!"

"Mrs. Potts?"

"Yes, dear. Now please, come right now, will you? I'm sure the police will want to see it if it *is* the bullet."

"Have you called them?"

"I'm not *sure* it is the bullet. I really hate to bother them again if it isn't, you see. Could you come now, do you suppose?"

Pete sighed, but supposed to Mrs. Potts that he could.

She greeted Pete at the door heavily coated and scarved and with a huge flashlight in her hand. "Oh, you are *so* reliable! Here it is. Now is that or is that not a bullet?" She held up a round, gray ball, approximately the size of a peewee marble, if Pete's memory of his peewees served him right. Pete hefted it, surprised at its weight.

"I've hunted and hunted for this bullet, Pete! Of course when Rita made me call the police the other day I knew it would do no good—no good whatsoever. They made the most *cursory* search. I found it right there in the woods! It took a considerable effort, I don't mind telling you. I'm not as nimble on my knees as I once was, and there really is a great deal of compost in the woods these days, isn't there? It really did take quite a bit of digging about. But there it was. What if it had hit one of my birds? What if one of my poor dear birds had swallowed it?"

Pete hefted it again. It looked and felt like lead, but it didn't look like any bullet he had ever seen. Then again, until recently, of course, he hadn't seen too many bullets.

"Now let me show you right where it was."

So this explained Mrs. Potts's coat and scarf. Pete followed her into the now black woods, wondering, not for the first time in his life, just how he got into these things. After thirty minutes of false trails and exclamations, the flashlight finally lit on a patch of ground the pigs must have been using to hunt for truffles.

"See?"

"I can hardly see my hand in front of my face, Mrs. Potts. I'll tell the police about this, but I'm sure in the morning—"

"Oh, you know how the police are, Pete. I call them quite a bit and I get very little satisfaction. Why, you remember what happened when I wanted them to arrest the Martells' cat for killing my birds? They absolutely refused to do a thing! Naturally when I heard the sniper firing in my woods I was most concerned about my chickadees. I always hang a seed wreath for my birds. I told Paul Roose that. I said I thought someone was trying to shoot my birds. The bullet whizzed by so close that it knocked the wreath right down. I picked it right up off the ground and showed him. And do you know he didn't say a word? Now this is where the sniper ran—right through the trees out there. I heard him. Now that I've found the bullet I'm sure there are some useful clues—"

"I'm sure tomorrow the police—"

"Oh, you're so good at this sort of thing, Pete. Why don't you take this bullet over to them? You could explain it all so much better than I. We don't communicate well, the police and I. As I said, I call them quite often."

Pete could imagine. "I'll take it over to them," said Pete, figuring it was the fastest way out—but he figured wrong.

"And while you're here. I've been meaning to call you. I need my Christmas boxes brought down from the attic. And my bathtub drain is stopped up again. And you really have to do something about the color on my television."

An hour later Pete drove straight from crazy Mrs. Potts's to Pease Street, but Connie's car was gone. He knocked anyway, trying to overcome a certain annoyance with her when there was no answer. What was he expecting after all—constant attendance to his every beck and call? Still, under the circumstances . . .

He went next to the police station. Jean Martell must have been able to tell that he was in no mood for her particular brand of inquisition. She fetched Paul Roose in record time.

This time Paul was a little more impressed, but not for the reasons Mrs. Potts supposed. "Forty-four-caliber lead ball. It's used with black powder, muzzle-loading guns. They've been obsolete since, oh, I'd say about the Civil War."

"*The Civil War?* What does *that* mean?"

"It means old Mrs. Potts made an archaeological find." Paul handed the lead ball back to Pete. "Here. Start a collection."

Pete was beginning to think he might. He drove down Shore Road to Pease Street again, but Connie's car was still gone. He began to wonder if at this rate he'd even see her before Christmas at all. He turned onto Shore Road and drove the long way around. He passed Connie's Triumph when he was almost to the causeway, looked in his rearview mirror, and saw her slow down.

Pete backed up and rolled down his window. "How about a beer?" he asked, wondering as he did so why Lupo's had suddenly become their safest ground.

"I'd love a beer."

Pete turned the truck around and they rode to Lupo's in tandem.

It seemed at first that Lupo's was just the right choice. They settled into a booth and commented on the crowd at the bar and ordered burgers and beer, and in the process of doing these trivial things Pete discovered that they *could* talk to each other. True, they were talking about things like hamburgers, but still, they were talking, and wasn't there such a thing as speaking between the lines? True, there was another one of those minutes when Abel Cobb's loud boasting about finding a redhead for Christmas threatened to weigh Pete down, but before he completely buried himself this time, Connie leaned across the booth and laughed.

"If he's grazing in these flesh-filled green pastures so goddamned much, why's he in here every night alone?"

Pete looked at the bar and noticed not Abel Cobb, but Nate Cox, just arriving. It didn't appear that Lupo's was Nate's first stop, either.

Pete and Connie talked on, continuing to speak between their own lines and to read between each other's, Pete could only hope correctly. One by one the barflies flew off, until Nate Cox was left sitting alone.

Pete watched Connie's face in the glow of the Santa candle as she talked, but he made no moves to leave, suddenly thinking that it wasn't *always* necessary to act. Sometimes it was more important not to break the spell.

The slight figure of Allison came through the door, saw Pete and Connie, ignored them, and headed straight to the bar to speak to her father. It was apparently to no avail. Nate Cox remained on his stool. Allison left.

It grew later. Pete looked at the clock, suddenly anxious over how late it was. It would be tomorrow soon. Seven more days till Christmas. He was rapidly getting his heart set on that Christmas fire and popcorn with Connie, alone. It would be their second chance. It would be the perfect setting for the settling of it all. It was time to speak, now. "Hey," he said. "About this going to New Jersey—"

"I'm not sure I'm going to New Jersey."

The answer he wanted to hear. Pete felt a hot rush of adrenaline in his veins. Yes, they were going to settle this Christmas business right now. He reached across the booth. "So what do you say? Want to—"

Up above them somewhere an explosion shattered their peace.

Dave Snow vaulted the bar, Pete and Connie ducked, Nate Cox swiveled in his seat with his mouth hanging open and his eyes stark with fright.

"Christ!" said Connie.

"Are you two all right?" hollered Dave Snow.

Pete and Connie nodded.

"What the hell was it?"

"The sniper," said Pete, looking at the empty hole up under the eaves.

This time Connie was out the door first, with him and Dave Snow only a step behind.

The night was warm, and a gray, musty-smelling fog hid any snipers as well as the water, the road, and even their own feet from view.

"I'm calling the cops," said Dave, returning inside. Pete and Connie followed him.

Nate Cox still sat on his bar stool, grinning now. "I

didn't do this. You three are a witness to it. I didn't do this!''

He was still saying it when the three policemen arrived one by one—first the chief, then Ted, and finally Paul Roose. He kept saying it as the chief meticulously questioned the four who had been inside.

Finally the chief took Pete aside. ''I don't want Cox driving. Take him home, will you?''

''I'll come back,'' said Pete. ''You'll need a lot of help trying to find anything in that fog.''

The chief shook his head. ''Don't bother. It'd take us all night to find anything out there.''

''Oh, yeah?'' Paul Roose walked up to the chief with a small cardboard tube in his hand. He tossed it in the air, caught it, and grinned. It didn't seem to be a very official way to handle evidence, and Pete, thinking about Cyrus's gun, wondered if there might be more to Paul's being stuck with desk duty than met the eye.

''Shotgun shell,'' said Paul. ''How do you like that for a little change of pace?''

Pete looked at the chief's face. He didn't look like he liked it much at all.

Together Pete and Connie shuffled Nate into the truck and home. Allison Cox opened the door to them apparently fresh from a shower, her hair damp and spiky, a white terry cloth robe clutched tightly around her, pink feet peeping out below. ''You didn't have to bring him home,'' she said.

''I didn't do it,'' said Nate.

''Of course you didn't.'' Allison grabbed her father's arm.

''There was another shooting tonight at Lupo's,'' Pete explained. ''Your father was still inside. He's feeling exonerated.''

''These are my witnesses.'' Nate waved a hand at

Pete and Connie. "Statements. They made statements. I didn't do it."

"Thank you," said Allison, easing her father into the room. "I'm sorry."

"No problem," said Pete. But he waited, not moving. Allison plopped her father onto the couch. At once he slipped sideways and lay awkwardly across the arm.

Pete looked at Nate's open mouth and closed eyes. "He's right, you know. No one's going to say he fired *this* shot."

Maybe it wasn't exactly tactfully put. Allison's face flushed red. She turned away. "Goodnight."

"No one was hurt," added Pete. "A lot of flying glass though. You might want to make sure he didn't get into any."

"Thank you," said Allison again, but not very politely. Clearly, she wanted them gone.

They went.

They drove in silence back to Lupo's to collect Connie's car. Pete pulled in next to the Triumph and hesitated, feeling the lack of that adrenaline that had been all set to help him out before. What now?

But before Pete could open his mouth Connie had already started across the day's mail, assorted bullets, old Cheetos, and other history that had collected between them on the seat of the truck.

Pete met her halfway.

Chapter
19

Connie sat up in bed and switched on the light.

"What," said Pete in that way he always did when rudely awakened from a sound sleep.

"I heard something." She slid her feet out of the bed but Pete reached out and caught her by the arm. He turned off the light. They lay in the dark and listened. After a minute she again tried to leave the bed and this time Pete came with her. She grabbed her coat off the chair, and behind her she heard Pete pulling on his pants. She padded across the bedroom, into the kitchen, and out onto the screened porch, with Pete right behind.

The fog had lifted and a three-quarter moon illuminated the long stretch of prickly lawn with the marsh and the sea beyond. A solitary deer moved over the grass in slow motion and into the scrub.

"Does he have a gun?" asked Pete.

Connie whirled around. "I don't think this is very funny! Who was in that bar tonight, anyway? You, me, Dave Snow, Nate Cox. Of all those people, who's the only one who was also at Sarah's and Beston's and the school, and who could have been expected to be on

Jerry's roof? I tell you, I think it's you this sniper is after. I think it's time you admit you're at risk and—''

"I wasn't at risk tonight."

"What in the holy hell are you talking about?''

Pete looked past her over the lawn. The deer was gone, but Pete seemed to think the moon over the still water was worth gazing at for a while. He went into the house and returned with the wedding ring quilt that Sarah Abrew had made for them when they got married. He stretched out on the porch glider and opened the quilt wide.

Connie sighed and slid in with him. It was cold enough to see their breath and to make being under the quilt with Pete the right place to be at just the right time.

Still, Connie got the strong feeling that she was the only one present who was really worried about the sniper, and she was determined to pound some sense into his noggin. Nobody else seemed to find Pete this stubborn. Was it her? Did she bring out the worst in him all the time? He kissed two of her favorite places. Okay, okay, maybe not *all* the time.

"Why won't you see reason about this? Who else could the sniper be after? Dave, me, Nate?''

"Okay. Why would the sniper be after me?''

Connie didn't answer that. It was true, she really couldn't think of any living person who could possibly want to harm Pete, but still, who else *could* the sniper be after?

"And besides," said Pete slowly, as if he were still thinking about it as he said it, "this was a shotgun tonight."

"So what? So people get bored using the same old gun all the time, so they go for a change. So what?''

Pete's body tensed against her. Christ, he was like some elephant who felt every single fly that landed on his skin, who never forgot which ones bit him. Suddenly Connie's own body was a bundle of knots.

"I don't give a damn what kind of gun he used. You could have been killed by tonight's shotgun as easily as you—"

"No," said Pete, once again in that musing kind of voice. "Not killed. Not tonight. Nobody could have gotten killed tonight. The sniper shot out the little window in the eaves. We were all at the other end. He could just have easily shot through the big windows and blown us full of holes, but he didn't."

Connie shivered, and that one shiver reminded her that she was lying outside in the middle of December with nothing but Sarah's quilt and Pete's body to keep her warm. She kept on shivering.

"Come on," said Pete. They returned inside, wrapped together in the quilt, and got back in between the sheets that had now turned cold.

"Still," said Connie. "I think you should be careful what you do, where you go." She almost told him again that she thought it would be best if he left right away for either the South or the North, but suddenly she couldn't stand the thought of him leaving her. She wanted to keep him near her to make sure that nothing else happened to him, that nobody would ever hurt him again. But wasn't that just the problem? Wasn't she the cause of all his pain? Wasn't his every third look like a look in her own mirror, reminding her that she was the last person in the world with whom he would find peace? Connie said nothing.

"Hey," said Pete, his voice already drowsy. "Tomorrow morning. First thing. We have to talk."

Pete fell asleep. Connie lay awake. At five o'clock she slipped out of bed and went home.

Pete ate his Wheaties the next morning with his head in a whirl. Not that he was complaining, mind you, but he hadn't got much sleep of late, and he wasn't thinking as clearly as he knew he should. First and foremost on his mind was Connie and whether what he thought was going on was really going on, and if it *was* really going on what exactly it all meant. Last night it had suddenly become so easy to be with her. Today he woke to find her gone. One way or another he was going to have to settle this! Today. Yes. He would ask her to spend Christmas with him. If she said yes, it would mean that their being together was the most important thing right now. If she said yes, then he'd say more. If she said no . . . Pete jabbed at a banana with his spoon. If he didn't tell his parents something soon they were going to book tickets and arrive on his doorstep. If he didn't tell Polly something soon she was going to go broke calling him up. Six days till Christmas. Too many decisions.

Too many *guns*. What *was* this last in a growing line of shootings all about, anyway? No one hurt. Four people scared. Was that what it was—a scare tactic? But who was supposed to be scared? And of what? Nate Cox? Connie? Pete? He couldn't seriously give any thought to the bartender, Dave Snow, who was there every night anyway and had been present at none of the other shootings. But then again, neither had Nate Cox! But if the condos were the issue it would leave out Nate Cox, since he would be the last person anyone rooting for the condos would want to scare away. And by no stretch of the imagination could he work Connie's presence into anything significant, although she had been present at Sarah's and—other than Newby, of course—closest to the fatal shot. She had also been present at Beston's and at the school. But Jerry's roof? True, she had arrived on the scene, but there could be nothing significant in that since no one could have known she would. And Connie had no relation to the condo issue, although a case might be made for the fact that, Connie being Connie, her views were certainly known.

That left Pete. But no. Pete couldn't see last night's shooting as relating to him at all. He wasn't at Lupo's all that often, and he was home, alone, a lot. If Pete were the target, the deserted road or beach that flanked Factotum would provide plenty of opportunity for a closer shot with much less risk. And Pete was not a person with a lot of enemies. When Pete was out of sorts he *usually* took it out on himself. By no stretch of the imagination could he think of anyone who would want to do him in. Or scare him off? But scare him off what—finding bullets and casings? But maybe someone was trying to scare him off *someone*. Pete stopped eating. The only person he was *on* was . . . No, not possible. He attacked his Wheaties again. He was getting nowhere by considering likely victims—maybe it was time to consider likely snipers instead. True, as far as last night was concerned, Nate Cox was out of the running. So who else? Who else had a shotgun, as well as a military rifle? Who had another choice of weapon to go to once he got "bored with one gun"? Pete's face began to burn. Yes, his guts still twisted and turned whenever he thought of Connie and Glen. Pete pushed away his breakfast and got up from the table. He wasn't going to think about Connie and Glen. Rifles. Shotguns. Think of those.

The first one of those Pete thought of was the shotgun in Cyrus Pease's barn.

Pete stopped at the police station first and caught Willy just heading out the door, looking grim. Since the chief didn't so much as slow his pace when Pete approached him, Pete fell in step and walked with him toward his Scout.

"Anything from last night?"

Willy stopped walking. "Connections," he said. "I want *connections*. I want the connection between Dillingham, Waxman, Beggs, the school, Lupo's. I want the connection between Cox and every one of these things, or Pease and every one of these things, or Dillingham and—''

"What if there isn't any?''

"There has to be. There already is. There are too many connections as it is now—that means there have to be a few more.'' Willy got into the Scout, slammed his door, and rolled down his window. "We were doing fine with Cox until he was inside the bar at Lupo's at the time of that last shot.''

"But that was different,'' began Pete.

Willy was too wound up to even hear him. "Since the sniper missed everyone at the school the connection is harder to draw. We don't have a specific target. Lupo's was a wild shot—so wild that maybe he wasn't even aiming to do anything but scare. I don't know. Those two don't worry me so much. But if I had something to tie Pease to Beggs . . .''

Willy drove off, still muttering.

Pete gave consideration to the police chief's little speech for about a mile's worth of Shore Road. Connections. Connections between one unsolved murder and four miscellaneous shootings, and connections tying one of the suspects to all of the crimes. Something about all this bothered him. The chief thought the connections that already existed were too many to ignore, but Pete thought there didn't seem to be enough. Not for Nashtoba. Not for murder, anyway.

When Pete drew abreast of Cyrus Pease's farm he noticed that Cyrus's barn doors were open wide, Christmas wreaths were hung in rows from the doors, and jugs of his famous cider were lined up on the small vegetable stand that he had pulled just inside the doors out of the wind. Pete pulled in.

Cyrus was sitting behind the stand, whittling a tiny reindeer out of island cedar.

Cyrus, who had seemed to be an obscure threat, if one at all, when the target had been only Newby and Evelyn, now seemed to be no threat at all in Pete's mind. What could possibly tie Cyrus to the shooting of Jerry Beggs, the blasts at the school and at Lupo's? Still, a murder weapon didn't necessarily have to belong to the murderer, did it?

"What's this," said Pete, "you're sticking around?"

"Till Saturday. Thought I might as well hang a few things on the old stand while I'm here. Chief came by about that tape. Told him what I told you. He didn't much like it, but there it is."

Pete was tempted to say that the chief didn't seem to like much these days, but he didn't. "You still can't pin down that voice?"

Cyrus shook his head. "Told him it might be Dillingham's."

"*Dillingham's?*"

"Told him it might not be, too." Cyrus sounded extremely regretful.

Pete was certain that he had heard that voice, or at least a distant cousin to it, but he didn't think it was Ozzie Dillingham's. It was hard to say, never having heard Ozzie when he wasn't hollering. But where else could he have heard that voice? He looked beyond the wreaths of cedar and bayberry to the empty hooks in the barn wall. "No more woodchucks around?"

Cyrus followed Pete's eyes to the wall and then jerked his head toward the house. "Locked up. I don't leave here with guns out loose."

Pete looked at the rusty padlock swinging open from the barn door hasp, a padlock that any old lady with a hairpin could probably pick. Pete circled the stand casually and came up closer to the place where the shotgun

169

had hung on the wall, but the bare rough-hewn boards told him nothing.

Pete returned to the front of the stand. Cyrus had finished the little reindeer and stood it on its fragile legs among the greens, its proudly held head and sorrowful eyes giving it a look that was half trapped, half free. It reminded Pete of Connie, and last night, and watching the deer on the lawn.

He bought a jug of cider for his parents, the little deer for Connie, and headed for Jerry Beggs's.

Betsy and Jerry were arguing. "Just who I wanted to see," said Betsy as she opened the kitchen door. "Remind this nut that he has a hole in his shoulder and a cracked rib, will you? He keeps trying to run off to the store." She swept Pete into the kitchen and pointed at Jerry, who was trying to shrug his bad shoulder into his coat alone.

"It was six days ago."

"Five!"

"Six. And it's six days till Christmas. If I don't get in there and deal with the deliveries, who knows what will—"

"You lift one box of books and you'll start bleeding all over again and really fix your ribs for good. Pete, talk to him. It was all I could do to keep him down off the barn."

"Isn't Allison scheduled for today?"

"She'll have her hands full with the register alone."

"So how about if I go with you? Just for today. I can drive, do any unpacking or lifting—you can check things out, make sure everything's okay."

Jerry's face brightened. Betsy frowned.

"Just today," Jerry repeated, and he was out the door before Betsy, or Pete, could catch him.

Pete enjoyed spending the day in Jerry's store. There was a coziness to the walls of books, a Christmasy air to the tinkle of the bell over the door and the red cheeks on the shoppers who breezed in from the cold.

Jerry was right—Allison was kept so busy ringing up sales that she didn't have time to distract Pete with her stares. Jerry was also right about the deliveries. Cartons of books were stacked in the aisles every which way. First Pete hauled all the boxes into the storeroom out back, and then he set to work with a razor, opening the cartons one by one. He found the perfect book for Polly—an anthology of New England ghost stories. Polly loved ghosts. Pete checked the books off against the order lists and stocked shelves, and when he finally straightened his aching back and looked at the clock it was past four. He walked up to the front of the store and saw that Jerry was white with strain. He hustled him into the truck and headed him home.

"Whew!" said Jerry. "I think I could use Factotum's whole crew, full time, for a week. Too bad I can't afford you."

"We could work in a few more hours. Sort of a combination Christmas-recuperation gift."

"No way. And besides, if I hire anyone else, I'm hiring Mary Pease."

Pete twisted around in his seat. "Mary Pease?"

"Mary asked Betsy in the fall, once the stand petered out, if we needed any help, and Betsy said no, but she promised to let her know if we changed our minds. Then Christmas came along and I got rushed and I forgot all about Mary and hired you guys on. Cyrus waltzed into the store a while back and there was Allison, and he said something to me like, 'Things must have picked up pretty suddenlike around here.' I felt pretty bad. I don't think the Peases have anything much to spare."

"Well, they have enough to go to Florida on," said Pete, but his mind was racing on from there. Could this be the Pease/Beggs connection the chief was yammering about? Could hold-a-grudge Cyrus have been that angry at Jerry to explain Jerry's shooting? Could this explain the episode at the school if Jerry were indeed the target there as well? Cyrus had the right kind of rifle and the old ammunition. Cyrus kept up. That left only Lupo's that didn't mesh. Lupo's. Lupo's and the shotgun. What if Cyrus's shotgun wasn't safely locked up inside at all? What if it *was* safely locked up inside but had been used in the shooting at Lupo's?

"I think their daughter sends them to Florida for Christmas every year," said Jerry, but Pete wasn't even listening.

Pete looked down at the seat of the truck and the little reindeer Cyrus had carved and suddenly he could see in its sad eyes much of the bitterness that Cyrus held over his lost land. The next minute he could see nothing in the delicate animal that a murderer could have created. No, thought Pete, Cyrus as murderer made no sense. If he said to Jerry that things must have picked up suddenly, that's all he meant—that he could see that things had picked up suddenly. Who'd hire Mary Pease at Christmas when she was going to leave for Florida any day?

But would hold-a-grudge Cyrus think of that? Didn't he make as much sense as murderer as any of the others? Who *could* make sense when you were talking about an *act* that made no sense? Nate Cox. Nate Cox made a lot of sense—if anything like this ever could, of course. Newby because of the condos. Evelyn because of the condos. Jerry because of his refusal to move his store into the condo mall. But still, that left the Lupo's shooting out, since Nate was inside being shot at himself.

So what about Ozzie, then? Ozzie killed his brother over condos? Ozzie killed Evelyn over condos? But why would Ozzie shoot at Jerry? Would Ozzie care if Jerry moved into the mall or not? Wouldn't Ozzie get his money either way? Would he get more if the mall were a going proposition on paper before the project actually began? Pete shook his head. With half a million dollars floating around, how much of a difference could one little bookstore make? A lot? Enough? No. He was clutching at straws, now, the same as the police chief was. Even if Jerry were enough of an obstacle for Ozzie, which Pete doubted, that still left out the shooting at Lupo's. There was no possible motive there. Did Ozzie even own a shotgun? Pete didn't know. Again, Lupo's was the odd crime out.

Suddenly Pete remembered who else had a shotgun, and a motive of sorts for some of the crimes. After Pete dropped Jerry off he headed for Shore Road to check on that other shotgun, but something—the reindeer on his seat, maybe—made him take a detour first.

Some instinct told Pete that right at the moment, his present need for a long, soul-searching talk with Connie aside, he would probably do better with her if he stuck to the formula that had been working so well at Lupo's last night: food. They'd pretty much exhausted all there was to say about hamburgers, so it was time to try another type of cuisine.

Two birds, one meal. He stopped off at his ex-wife's and asked her out on a date. Dinner at Martelli's for two.

Chapter
20

Connie sat across from Pete at Martelli's and picked at her eggplant parmesan, trying not to notice the other people in the room. Every third eye in the place was staring at them and whispering between the tines of their forks, and there were only about six eyes in the whole place anyway. So big deal! So she and Pete were eating dinner. Christ, what a place!

"So tell me again," said Connie, somewhat peevishly, she knew. It seemed so dumb to be sitting here with Pete after all this time and to be talking about nothing but guns. Were guns a step up or a step down from hamburgers? But she kept doing it, and he kept going along with it. Which one of them was more afraid of what they would say or hear next? Connie wiped sweaty palms on her thighs and started again.

"Alton Martell had a shotgun, right here at his restaurant, and you want to find out if it's still here without asking him right out, is that it? But hell, I still don't see where Lupo's fits—not with this place, not with anything."

"That's the problem," said Pete. "Lupo's doesn't fit. Wrong gun. But still, it was a shooting and we should find the gun. I don't think it's advisable to ask Willy to look into it just yet. I don't think it has anything to do with Alton, but still, what if the gun is gone? Anyone could have taken it—it's lying right out in plain sight.''

"Not plain sight," said Connie, who had been shown, from the door, just where the gun was supposedly stashed. She pushed her plate away, not so hungry of late for some reason. "Okay, how about this? when we leave, we go find Alton in the office. You walk him outside to ask him something about his addition, I'll say I'm going to the ladies' room, and once you and Alton leave I look behind the desk for the gun.''

"Maybe you should get Alton away and I'll look for the gun.''

"What am I supposed to do, ask him if he wants a quickie in the backseat?" The minute the words were out Connie knew that she had once again run afoul of Pete's spiderweb of traps by the deep freeze that settled in around his mouth. For Chrissake, was she going to have to watch every word she said for the rest of her life? Had he lost his memory as well as his sense of humor? Pete and Connie would go to a drive-in movie in the truck and he'd say that to her—How about a quickie in the backseat? The truck didn't have a back-seat. It had been a joke then, it had been a joke now. "The *back*seat," she said again. Get it? *Get it?*

Pete continued to sit there stiff as the Sphinx. "I'll talk to Alton," he said. They finished the meal without speaking another single, solitary word.

The other portion of the evening was more sucesssful. The shotgun was right where it was supposed to be, and Connie was leaning against the office door, supposedly newly returned from the ladies' room, when Pete and Alton returned from outside.

"The office looks nice, Alton," said Connie. "New furniture?''

Alton pointed at Pete. "Factotum refinished it all. Allison brought back the last broken drawer this morning." He waved at the long mahogany sideboard against the wall.

Pete's head snapped around. "Drawer? Allison?"

"It was broken. She and Andy brought the furniture back yesterday, but last night Allison came to collect one of the drawers. She said it wasn't square and wouldn't slide right. But she brought it back this morning all fixed and it works fine. Tell them both to stop by for a free feed some night, will you, Pete?"

Pete didn't answer him. "Let's go," he said to Connie, and hurried them out the door.

"I'm telling you," Pete kept telling her once he had returned her to her apartment. "The shooting at Lupo's is the one thing that doesn't fit. Not the weapon, not the possible victims, not the nature of the shot itself."

"But *Allison?*"

"What was the one thing that shooting did? It eliminated Nate Cox as a suspect. That's the only thing it did—it didn't do a damned thing else. It didn't come close to hurting anyone else. She came in, she saw him obviously cemented for a while to the bar, she saw you and me—a couple of handy witnesses. She went to Martelli's somehow and scoffed up the gun. She came back and blasted through the little window at the far end, away from all of us, making sure she didn't hurt anyone at all. She could have taken her father's gun, but that would have added more to his plate, even if he *was* inside the bar at the time. So she took Alton's. She didn't care if it was a different gun—she knew no one would ever believe there were two snipers loose. We almost didn't."

"But *Allison?*"

"Didn't she seem strange to you when we brought

Nate home? She didn't even ask what happened. She didn't even ask if anyone was hurt. She knew damned well what had happened, and she knew no one was hurt!"

"She was all wet. She was just out of the shower."

"She was all wet. Nobody said anything about a shower. The fog was wet. She got soaked in the fog. So she threw on her robe and we assumed she was fresh out of the shower. I happen to know she showers every morning—she comes in with her hair soaking wet every day."

"So she showered twice. Big deal."

Pete just looked at her.

"Okay, so how did she get the gun in and out with no one seeing her?"

"In that long drawer. Allison wasn't even working on that furniture—Andy was. There was no reason for her to be mucking around with the drawer."

"But would Allison do that for her father?"

"She half supports him, I know that. She lies for him, too. I know that. She keeps saying he wasn't in the action in the war. Nate himself says otherwise. She gave him an alibi that the police think is a lie as well."

"So maybe she did *all* the shootings."

"I don't think so. It only makes sense if she thinks her father did the others, if she thinks he needs witnesses for an alibi for one more."

"So *did* he do the others?"

"Of the choices . . ." began Pete, but he didn't finish the thought. It wasn't an easy thing to do, to select a murderer out of a group of people you knew.

"So what now?"

"I have to see Willy. He'll have to check out Alton's gun."

"Now? You'll have to see Willy now?"

Pete nodded.

Connie looked at the clock, half relieved. She was beat, as she seemed to be every time she was confronted with whatever Pete kept silently confronting her with these days.

Like right now. There he sat, watching and waiting, expecting her to ask him to come back later. If she asked him to come back, there she was at Go. If she *didn't* ask him . . .

She yawned. Just like that, an if-you're-not-asking-*me*-back-who-*are*-you-asking look came to his eye.

Connie yawned again.

"Okay." Pete was no dummy. "We'll call it a night. But tomorrow we should talk. After school. We need to settle some things."

What could you settle with someone who still had her "quickie in the backseat" floating around behind his eyes?

"I have a meeting after school."

"After the meeting."

"It's a long meeting."

"So Saturday, then."

No, he wasn't going to let this drop. The best she could do was to opt for neutral territory—someplace she could leave cleanly when she failed to pass Go. "So meet me at Lupo's at eight."

Hell, maybe the sniper would get her first.

Suddenly Connie felt a little sick to her stomach.

Maybe the sniper would get *him* first.

Pete looked at her strangely. He walked over to her and kissed her strangely. It reminded Connie of one of those scenes in the old forties movies she and Pete used to watch, the scene with the classic kiss good-bye.

Chapter
21

Pete left Connie's apartment feeling extremely out of sorts. Things were going all wrong. He wasn't any closer to settling things about Christmas. He wasn't getting the chance to say what he wanted to say. Connie, on the other hand, was saying plenty, but none of it was what he wanted to hear. *A quickie in the backseat.* Pete didn't even *have* a backseat! There were others who did, of course. Glen, for example.

And clearly she didn't want to have this little talk. Or anything else, either. Yawning. Right. Why, because she knew he wanted to get things onto firm ground by Christmas? Didn't she want that? No, apparently not. What did she want—to go home to New Jersey? To bolt? *Again?* Yes. Clearly.

Pete swung past the chief's house, but the house was dark and the Scout was gone. He planned to go straight to the station, but somewhere along the way he remembered a pair of large gray eyes and thought again.

After all, didn't Allison deserve a chance to hear it from him first? True, it was too late to go to her house tonight, but it wasn't as if anyone else were in danger from her. She had taken care not to hurt a fly, she had given her father the alibi he needed—she had no reason to do the same stupid thing again. Couldn't it wait till morning, when he could talk to her first, go with her to the station if she chose to do so? Give her that chance to go in voluntarily. Another chance. She might be the only one who was going to get one this year!

Pete went home.

The phone was ringing when he got in.

Pete glared at it, but after a long series of rings he snapped it up. "Hello."

"Well, for crying out loud. Sound a little glad to hear from me, can't you?"

"Hello, Polly," Pete repeated.

"Whoa! Can I stand all this Christmas glee?"

"So what's so gleeful about it? This whole holiday's about a very depressing subject. Pregnant women being denied hotel rooms. Parents placing unrealistic expectations on their child. I don't see why we're supposed to be so *happy* about it all."

There was a considerable span of silence from the other end of the phone. "And here I am trying to spend Christmas with *you*. What am I, nuts?"

"Yes," said Pete. "You are."

"So you're not coming?"

"I don't know. If you have to know today, the answer's no."

"And here Mom called and begged me to talk you off that island. She thinks you hate Florida. And she thinks you're going to get shot."

"I'm not going to get shot."

"So don't sound so disappointed. Really, Pete. Come on up. You can show up anytime. Christmas Eve. Christmas Day. Just wear a red suit, carry a bag with lots of presents, say, Ho ho ho—"

"Ho ho ho," said Pete.

This time the pause was even longer. "It's Connie, isn't it?"

"No."

"Want me to ask her up here, too?"

"No," said Pete fast. That's all he needed, Polly beaming at them the whole time.

"All right. So tell me about this sniper."

It did occur to Pete that it was a little strange to feel so continually relieved once the subject of murder came up. He filled Polly in. He talked a long time, going over all the old ground as well as his new thoughts. When he finished, Polly concentrated on the gaps.

"So you either need a reason for Ozzie to kill Jerry or, if Mom's right, for one of them to kill you. If you're as much of a Grinch around there as you are over the phone, it's clear enough why any of them would want to kill *you*. Jerry, though, I don't know. Ozzie does hate books, but somehow I don't think that's going to cut it."

"What do you mean, he hates books?"

"Oh, Newby said Ozzie used to get on his case every time Newby wanted to read instead of play cards. He said Ozzie used to say all the evils of the world were born in books—just look at *Mein Kampf*. If Hitler hadn't written it, he wouldn't have felt so obliged to prove his point."

Pete laughed.

"Oh, God," said Polly. "You *are* a mess if Hitler cheers you up. I'm getting off this phone before I catch it. Good-bye."

"Good-bye," said Pete.

It was true. He was a mess. It was also true that Hitler *had* cheered him up. Ozzie had seen action at Leyte, Mindoro, Luzon, and Okinawa. Jerry Beggs had been a conscientious and vociferous objector to the Vietnam War. Maybe Ozzie resented that. Newby would have been too young for World War II—maybe Ozzie resented that as well. Wasn't Newby killed on December seventh, Pearl Harbor Day? And Pete knew Evelyn Waxman was a pacifist by nature. Maybe . . . But why was Pete trying so hard all of a sudden to pin this on Ozzie—because he charged him tourist rates? No. He wasn't trying to pin this on Ozzie—he was trying to figure this damned thing out. And when all was said and done, what *had* Pete figured out? Nothing except Allison.

Pete went to bed and dreamed that Connie gave him a rifle for Christmas just before she left to go live in Taiwan and that he shot Allison with it by mistake.

Things hit the fan fast and furiously the next morning. The first big cog in the works was Maxine, who flagged him down bright and early at the corner on his way to Sarah's. Against his better judgment, Pete swung open the truck door and Maxine scrambled in.

"What are you doing here? You're supposed to be in—"

"School. I *know* that." She rolled her eyes—big brown ones that reminded Pete very much of her mother's, especially when they were rolling, but Pete knew better than to say that to her face.

"I just want to *ask* you something, all right?"

"Sure." Pete eased the truck forward, deciding to head somewhat surreptitiously in the general direction of school.

"I just want to ask you if you're sticking around here, that's all. Every time I see you my mom's right there. I mean, are you going someplace for Christmas or anything? Mom says you might not."

"I might not. I don't know yet. You're going to Aunt Ethel's?"

Maxine shrugged and seemed to slump lower in the

seat. Her short black hair, very much like her mother's in color but not in style, plumed up against the back of the seat. "Well, I just wanted to know if you were going to be here, that's all."

Pete opened his mouth to ask why, but he was pretty sure he knew why. He could see it now—Pete and Maxine here for Christmas, Rita fuming at Aunt Ethel's. His head began to ache.

"I wouldn't count on me," he said. "Is Aunt Ethel—"

"Aunt Ethel, Aunt Ethel!" Maxine shouted suddenly. "I don't *want* to go to Aunt Ethel's! I want to stay here near Todd! And Mom won't let me stay alone!"

Pete pulled to a stop in front of the school.

"I just don't know, Max."

Maxine opened the truck door, slid out, and slammed the door so hard that Pete looked for it in his rearview mirror as he drove off.

His headache got worse at Sarah's.

"I don't see why they're making such a fuss about it," she said, stomping with her cane between the bedroom and the dining room, where her suitcase was half packed and open on the table. "All this work. All this packing. All this *phoning* all the time. In my day we wrote letters. In my day we stayed put! I think it's foolish that I'm going to Joanna's at all. As a matter of fact, why am I? No, I don't think I will. I'm too tired. It's too much work." She slapped shut the cover of the suitcase, marched into the living room, and sat down. "So are you going to read to me or not?"

Pete sat down on the couch, opened up the paper, and rubbed his aching head. " 'Cape readies for New Year's Eve Fest,' " he read.

"Now there," said Sarah. "Why traipse halfway across the earth? There'll be plenty to do right here."

* * *

When Pete returned to Factotum, Allison and Andy had just arrived, and Rita was sorting out the day's tasks between them.

"Allison, you're scheduled at the Bookworm today. Andy, you're wrapping Christmas presents for the Hendersons."

"A minute," said Pete to Allison before she could follow Andy out the door, and she turned in surprise. "Do you have a minute?" He waved toward the hall.

Allison said nothing. She hardly even looked at him this time. She followed him back down the hall to his kitchen, and when he waved at one of the chairs at the kitchen table, she sat. Pete sat in the other. He tried to think of an oblique way to begin.

"Did you fire the shot at Lupo's?" he asked.

She started to cry. Everything turned red on Allison when she cried—face, scalp, eyes, nose, even her hands as she brought them up to her face to cry into them.

"I don't mean to upset you," Pete stumbled on, "but the thought did occur to me. You certainly knew your father was there and you certainly have been concerned that he's been under some suspicion. Was that it—to divert the suspicion from your father? He seemed to think it worked, didn't he? And you didn't seem surprised, Allison. You didn't even ask if anyone was hurt. This wasn't done with the sniper's gun, and it wasn't done with the sniper's mind, I don't think. It was done with a mind that was very careful *not* to hurt anyone."

Allison kept on crying. Pete got up to get her some water, wondering as he did so why you always jumped up to get water for people who were upset. Weren't they more likely to choke? As he lingered, filling up the glass, and strolled in a leisurely fashion to the refrigerator for the ice, he suddenly figured it out. You gave water to people so that *you'd* have something to do. But it didn't give you *enough* to do. Pete returned to the table, his head pounding, to find Allison standing by the door.

"You used Alton Martell's shotgun, didn't you?"

Allison looked at Pete. It was a look that was painful to receive. Pete moved closer, holding out the water.

"I'm trying to help you. Believe me, you're going to get found out. You've probably already been found out. I wanted to talk to you first, so that you could go to the police yourself instead of waiting for them to come to you. This isn't going to help your father at all—can't you see that? Can't you see that all you're doing is convincing everyone that you think your father's guilty?"

The next thing Pete knew, Allison was crying in his arms. Or arm. He balanced his sacred water precariously behind her back until the sobs lessened, then pushed her gently away.

"I'll be right back, then I'll go with you to the station."

Pete left the room to get some aspirin. When he came back, Allison was gone.

Chapter
22

Rita looked up at the sound of Pete's sneakers drumming over the pine floors.

"Where'd she go?" he hollered.

"Who?"

"Allison. *Allison*. She was just here. She was just *in there*." He waved an arm wildly behind him.

"She left. I assumed she was on her way to Jerry's."

"She didn't say where she was going? Was she crying? Did she seem upset? She didn't say she was going to the police?"

Rita stared at Pete. "*No*, she didn't say she was going to the police. What's all this about?"

"I think she was the one who shot out the window at Lupo's. I told her so. I was talking to her, trying to reason with her, trying to get her to go to the police, but I left the room for one minute—*one minute*—and now she's gone! Was she crying?"

"I don't *know*," Rita repeated crossly. "She went down the hall with you. She came out. I didn't *notice* if she was crying. I didn't know you'd been accusing her of a *crime*."

"I'm going to Jerry's," said Pete. He charged over and yanked open the door. "And who put up this wreath?"

Rita glared right at him, but she found she was glaring at the rear of him. He was already gone.

Pete raced to Jerry's and banged open the shop door, oblivious this time to any mood-enhancing qualities to the jingle of the little bell. Jerry was behind the counter, peering through his half glasses at the inside jacket corner of a trade paperback edition of Dickens's *A Christmas Carol*. "Seven ninety-five, forty cents tax, eight thirty-five," he said to his customer. Allison was nowhere in sight.

"Isn't Allison here?"

"No, she didn't show. I came in to take care of a few things and ended up manning the register instead."

"Can you get by okay for a bit?"

"Sure I can. I'm doing fine. Just don't tell Betsy."

"Will you call me if Allison comes in? If you can't get me, call Willy McOwat. Okay?"

Jerry removed his glasses and looked harder at Pete. "If Allison comes you want me to call the cops?"

Pete gritted his teeth. "Me. If Allison comes, call me. Only call Willy if you can't get me or if you think she's going to leave again, okay?"

"I suppose someday you'll explain yourself?"

"You'll have to wait in line," said Pete bitterly, and he charged back out the door, glaring at the bell as it jingled again.

Once back in his truck, Pete hesitated. He didn't want to go to the station if it were at all possible to corral Allison first. There was a right way and a wrong way to do these things. Granted, Allison was well down the road to doing it the wrong way, but Pete wanted to try to reverse that trend if he possibly could. Where else

187

would she possibly go? Pete had just accused her of trying to protect her father by shooting out the window at Lupo's. He had also just told her it hadn't worked. Where would she go after that—home?

Home.

Maybe.

Pete walked into the real estate office, and there was Nate Cox, sitting behind the desk, staring down at his own rough, red hands. As Pete entered, he looked up with little interest.

"Is Allison here?"

Nate got a little more interested. "Here? No. I thought she went to work."

"She came and went. She didn't come back here?"

Nate shook his head, definitely interested now. "I know she didn't go in the other day, I talked to her about that. Seemed to be a little annoyed with you. But she went in today. She never said—"

"It's important that I find her. I think she's done something against the law to try to protect you, and if she takes off it's going to make things much, much worse."

"Protect *me?*"

Pete sighed. "Listen, Nate. I think Allison fired that shot at Lupo's. I think she did it to divert suspicion from you, since you were inside. I talked to her about it and she burst out crying and bolted on me. I think she should go to the police herself, before they come to her, don't you? Do you know where she might be?"

Nate Cox looked at Pete for a long time, and Pete could almost see his thoughts flash back and forth inside his head. Allison. Lupo's. Crying. Where? "She wouldn't do that."

"She's already lied for you. She's already told the police that you spent the war behind a desk and couldn't fire an accurate shot to save yourself. She also gave you an alibi. Did she lie about that, too?"

Nate Cox finally became a little more action oriented. He stood up. Pete tensed. *Was* this guy the sniper? If so, would he now be counting up what, if anything, he had to lose? Nate's face was a battleground of emotions. Which would win?

"Allison never lied in her life."

"The guys at Beston's told me you were an expert marksman. You told me yourself you saw considerable action in the war. I don't see how you can—"

To Pete's surprise, Nate Cox crashed back into his chair and burst out laughing. He reached into his pocket and threw his wallet onto the desk.

"You're looking in the wrong place for the liar," he said. "Here." With shaky fingers he dug through the cards and pieces of paper in his wallet, selecting one. He tossed it to Pete. "Look at the enlisted record side. Eighth line down."

Pete looked impatiently at the clock. He was going to have to go from here to the police station—he had stalled around with this long enough. He looked at the card: EXP. RIFLE.

"Right. Expert. And Allison says—"

"Allison says right. Oh, I flashed that card around at the store when I first came here, when those old fellows were trying to break me in. The only thing I hit in the war was the wastepaper basket. With a wad of paper. Expert marksman? My good pal Frank Lake was in the target pit when we had to qualify on the rifle range. I missed the target every time, should have gotten the red flag, Maggie's drawers. What did he do? Chalked me up to bull's-eyes. Expert marksman." Nate Cox balled up his discharge paper and hit the wastebasket on the first try. "Big joke. I was afraid to correct the misapprehension—I thought it might get Frank in trouble. Expert marksman, here I am."

"But what about those stories you told in the bar?"

Nate laughed again. "Oh, you young fellows were ticking me off. I decided to tell a few tales of my own. I guess I picked a bad time."

"I guess you did. But Allison picked what she thought was a very good time. She shot out the window at Lupo's and she ran."

Finally Nate Cox seemed to realize the importance of what Pete had been saying all along. He jumped to his feet. "Where is she?"

"I was hoping you could tell me. Since you can't, I can't wait around any longer. I have to see the chief." Pete moved fast for the door.

"It was just a window!" Nate called after him. "They won't do anything to her for just a window! It wasn't like she was the one who did all the rest!"

Pete stopped at the door. "I happen to think you're right about that. That's why I waited to talk to her, before going to the police. I wanted her to go to the police and explain what she'd done. That's why I was hoping you'd know where she'd gone."

Nate Cox pulled a coat on over a threadbare sweater. "I don't know where she is, but that red Chevette of hers shouldn't be hard to spot. We can do that first, can't we—circle the island and look for her car before you go to the police?"

Pete considered. It seemed like a bad idea on all counts. For all he knew he'd be driving around the island with the very man who *had* done all the rest. But then again, from what he knew about the sniper so far, driving around beside him in daylight was probably one of the safest places to be. Pete nodded. "One quick swing around, then I go to the station."

"One quick swing," Nate promised.

Pete forgot he was dealing with a known fabricator of facts.

Every time Pete decided they'd covered all the logical spots, Nate thought up yet another one, and Pete was surprised at his intimate knowledge of the island's ins and outs. When finally there seemed to be nothing left on the island to explore, Nate whined and cajoled until Pete agreed to cross the causeway and head for Bradford to check out the airport, bus terminal, and train station.

"But does she have enough money for a trip?" asked Pete.

Nate Cox gave a laugh. "She does better off you than I do off this whole island. She could sure take a long bus ride, or at least a short hop in a plane."

They tried the bus station first, the train station second, the airport last. Her car was parked at the tiny municipal airport, but no one of Allison's description had recently boarded a plane.

"Maybe she left the car here to confuse us and then took off for the bus station. Or the train station."

They doubled back over their tracks, this time displaying at each ticket booth a picture of Allison that Nate had dragged out of his wallet. Allison's gray eyes, tiny bones, and cropped hair stared out of the picture silently, much the way she did in real life. The picture could have been taken ten years ago or ten days ago. It could never have been taken at all, for all the good it did them. They batted zero each time.

"Okay, that's it, Nate," said Pete. "Back to the police station."

"If we could just try one more—"

"That's *it*," snapped Pete. He'd gone way too far out on a limb as it was. "Something might have happened to her—didn't you think of that? The police have to know."

It was a tough way to do it, but it shut Nate up.

*   *   *

Willy McOwat was not so quiet. He hollered his head off at the two men, but mostly at Pete, for a good minute and a half, all the while radioing out a description of Allison and ordering Ted to Martelli's restaurant to pick up Alton's gun.

"Cyrus has a shotgun too," said Pete. "He says it's locked up in his house with the other guns now, but it used to be hanging out in the barn with a rusty padlock on the door."

"We'll check on that too. She could have gotten the shotgun from the same place she got the rifle before."

Nate Cox paled.

"Do you mean it was Cyrus's gun that did the other snipings?" asked Pete. "You've heard from the lab?"

The chief shook his head. "We heard from the lab. It wasn't Cyrus's rifle. We're still looking for the weapon." Here he looked hard at Nate.

"Wait a minute," said Pete. "Nobody said Allison fired anything but that one shot at Lupo's—the one that didn't fit. There's no reason for her to—"

"Then why'd she run?"

"We don't *know* she ran," said Pete lamely, looking at Nate Cox.

Nate seemed unable to speak.

"And besides, what's Allison's motive?"

"The same as yours," said Willy, turning on the realtor once again. "Or more. She feels this place has denied you your dignity, your God-given right to make a buck. Do you happen to have a picture of your daughter around?"

Without a word Nate Cox opened his wallet and extracted the picture that he and Pete had used earlier.

"What are you going to do?" asked Pete quickly, before Nate Cox could either think or speak.

192

"I'm going back to the car to check that out first, then I'm going to track her down."

Willy headed out, his massive shoulders swinging one after the other through the door, his leather holster creaking. Pete thought of the bulk of the police chief and the toothpick that was Allison Cox. He winced.

Pete took Nate Cox back to his office and then stopped at Beston's Store. He went inside, bought a cup of coffee, and ambled in the direction of the conversation around the stove.

"Now me, I get the wife something she can put to good use," said Bert. "This year I got her this gas barbeque grill that—"

"I thought *you* handled the grill, Bert," said Ed Healey.

"Well, she *eats* the stuff, doesn't she?"

Evan Spender winked at Pete. "I'd like to think you're pulling our leg, Bert," said Ed, "but something tells me you aren't."

"Just the way you were pulling my leg about Nate Cox being an expert marksman?" asked Pete. "I knew there was a joke there—I just didn't know what it was. Who told you he wasn't?"

"Allison," said Ed. "She was in here not long ago, and Bert started hassling her about her father being the big expert shot. She got mad and told us the truth. Pretty funny."

Pete was having a hard time thinking so. He wondered how fast Willy would find her. He wondered what Willy's philosophy was about giving people another chance.

Pete went up to the counter and bought his parents Beston's special coffee beans and the mulled cider mix they offered at Christmas. George Beston had festooned the wall behind the cash register with wreaths made out of lottery tickets. Pete bought a season's ticket for Sarah. He figured it was the most chances anybody around here was going to get.

Chapter 23

Pete made five calls to the station that day, talked to Jean Martell twice and Paul Roose the remaining three times. Each time Pete called the news was the same. There wasn't any. The chief wasn't back; Allison had not been found. Each time he called the station he became a little bit more depressed. Each time he talked to another human being, he sank lower and lower under the various weights of the world they kept heaping upon his shoulders.

The first weight was Rita's.

"Is there *anything* you can say to that child to make her snap out of this before she ruins everyone's Christmas? She listens to you. Can't you say *something?*"

"She wants to be with Todd."

"*Todd* hasn't even asked her to stay! She wants me to leave her here *alone*, at *home*, so she can *stop in* on Todd Christmas Eve! You see how senseless that is? Will you *talk* to her, please?"

"If I see her," said Pete, which was clearly not what Rita had wanted him to say.

The second weight was Sarah's—or rather, her daughter Joanna's, who called Pete from Baltimore.

"Pete, please, you have to do something about my mother. Now she says she's not coming."

So let her alone, Pete wanted to say. "So what can I do?" he asked instead.

"Talk to her. It's all planned. She gets like this—you know her. It's just the idea of being uprooted. It's happened other years—I'm sure you remember."

Yes, and there had been other years when Sarah had stayed on the island and had a very merry Christmas with Pete.

And Connie.

"I'll talk to her," said Pete. "But I don't always come out ahead when I do that, Joanna."

"If anyone can come out ahead it's you—you know that."

No, Pete didn't, but he promised to try. Joanna wished him a Merry Christmas, to which Pete responded with a mumble of some sort.

And then there was the call from his mother.

"Oh, Peter," she said first thing into the phone. The use of the full name was a very depressing sign. It meant that she was planning on being very mothery. "I just don't know what to do about you. If I'd thought for a minute when we changed our plans that I might not be seeing you at Christmas, I . . ."

"I'll tell you Sunday for sure, one way or the other, if I'm coming or not."

"You'll *never* get a plane at this late date."

"So I'll drive down. If I decide to. I'll tell you Sunday for sure." By Sunday he would know, one way or the other. Tomorrow was Saturday, and tomorrow night, when he saw Connie, he was going to straighten things out. One way or the other. By Sunday he'd know something, whether it was what he wanted to know or not.

Pete decided to escape the phone. He went to Hansey's and bought Andy a pair of work boots with steel-reinforced toes. He bought Allison a thick wool sweater that was heavy enough to slow her down, hoping that a file in a cake wouldn't prove to be of more use. He decided not to buy Connie anything else until they'd had their talk the following night. Four shopping days till Christmas. For now, his was done.

Pete lay awake that night trying to figure out what exactly he wanted to say to Connie the next night and what exactly he wanted her to say to him. He decided it would be best just to start with Christmas. If she stayed with him for Christmas, there would be plenty of time to say the rest. That settled at 2:30 A.M., he closed his eyes with a sigh.

Then the ghosts started in. From 2:30 A.M. until 3:30 A.M. he reviewed the special moments of past Christmases he and Connie had shared. From 3:30 A.M. until 4:00 A.M. he went over every painful detail of the Christmas they had spent apart. From 4:00 A.M. until 5:00 A.M. Pete reexamined his behavior at each of their meetings to date. At 5:05 A.M. Pete decided he was a jerk, and he lay awake from 5:06 A.M. until 6:59 A.M. collecting further evidence to support his case. At seven he had just about decided on elective frontal lobotomy as the only means of achieving a good night's sleep. He got up and called the station.

Paul Roose informed him that Allison was still unaccounted for and that Nate Cox was hanging around the station getting on everyone's nerves. Pete wanted to ask Paul what the hell he was doing answering the phone if Allison was still unaccounted for. Shouldn't he be out looking? He also wanted to ask if a sniper would be likely to hang around a police station.

Instead, Pete left for Sarah's.

Sarah was in a swell mood. She just wasn't going to go to her daughter's for Christmas.

"They think they have to have me every year. They don't have to have me *every* year. It's nice they ask, but I think it's better I say no once in a while. I don't need to see them to have a good time. Everyone thinks you have to be around your family to have a nice time. Sometimes I think it's the reverse!"

"Did you ever stop to think that maybe they need to be around *you* to have a nice time?"

Sarah blinked at him. "No," she said. "But if they do, they'd better practice doing without."

"You're not giving them a lot of notice, Sarah. It's only four days away. And what about all your baloney about Christmas meaning another chance? You're going to pass up one of those chances, is that what you're telling me?"

"There's no sense telling you anything, since you never listen anyway," she snapped. "Now what's all this about shotguns, now?"

Pete filled her in. When he was through, Sarah got up without speaking and stumped out of the room on her cane. She stumped back in without it, leaning on the butt end of a gun.

"This was my husband, Arthur's. He's been dead forty-five years. I think it's paid tribute to his memory long enough. Get rid of it, Pete."

No, Nashtoba's not a gun place.

Pete didn't have the faintest idea what you did with old guns. Did you just throw them out? He decided to deliver Sarah's shotgun into the hands of the police.

The particular hands available at the moment were, of course, Paul Roose's.

"Still no Allison?"

"Still no Allison," Paul answered.

* * *

When Connie walked through the door at Lupo's well after eight o'clock, Pete's initial annoyance at her lateness was swept away by the sight of her, and fully reinstated seconds later by the swiveling heads of Abel Cobb, Wally Melville, and even Dave Snow at the bar.

Not that Pete could blame them. One dismissive glance from Connie's green eyes was enough to wake them all up, and her long, open coat, nondescript jeans, and bulky sweater may have left everything to the imagination, but there was something about her that caused the imagination to run wild. Then Pete saw the arrogantly raised chin and knew that he alone knew what that particular posture meant. She was at a low ebb. Why? Because she had come to meet a jerk.

Pete half stood as she slid into the booth across from him, not from any outdated courtesy, but because his inner turmoil was such that he had to move or burst. He tried to push aside his irritation at Connie for being late, at the men at the bar for admiring her, at himself for being such a jerk when he was around her. It was time to speak.

"I've tried so hard not to love you," he said.

The chin quivered and rose higher still. "I suppose that's better than having to try to do the reverse. Me, I don't seem to try to do anything at all, but there it is. Still."

"I want to know—"

There was a roar at the bar, and Pete looked up to see Abel half beached across it, hands reaching for Tina Hansey, who stood behind it. Wally Melville pulled him back. Pete looked at Connie again, but she just sat there with her chin up, as if waiting for him to take his next swing.

"These times with you this past week. We did all right. We . . ."

Abel Cobb roared again, and despite himself, Pete

looked again. This time Dave Snow and Wally Melville were escorting him out the door.

Pete fell helplessly silent. He wanted Connie to say something. He felt it was up to *her* to say something. *She* was the one who had walked out. He watched her, but she was looking out the window now, watching Wally shove Abel into his car and climb in after him to drive him home.

"He must be awfully lonely if he comes in here every night," she said.

Pete felt that old tick of anger. Was that all she had to say? "If he's lonely, it's his own fault. He could be home having Christmas with his wife and his kids."

"Oh, really?" said Connie. "I've found out a few things about Abel since we were here last. His wife tossed him out on his ear. She's got some lawyer who's going to marry her after he bleeds Abel dry. He's fixed it so Abel's not allowed to access their accounts or to see his kids. That's why he quit his job—that's why he's had to come back here to sell the house."

"It doesn't sound like he's been too lonely."

Connie blinked her eyes. "You really *believe* that? Abel Cobb, the stud of the eastern seaboard? Can't you see he's just trying to pretend he's someone Wally and Dave and you or anyone else who's listening won't think is a loser? Someone *he* won't think is a loser?"

"You seem to know a lot about Abel."

Connie slammed two balled-up fists onto the table, and to Pete's horror her eyes filled with tears. "I know a hell of a lot about losers. I lost everything. *Everything.*"

She stood up, scrambling for her coat, not waiting to put it on but dragging it behind her across the barroom floor. Pete jumped up, fumbled enough money onto the table for the beers only he had drunk, and ran after her out the door. She saw him behind her. She ran past her car and onto the beach, her coat and hair floating out behind her as she ran.

"I came here to tell you I want you back!" Pete shouted after her into the wind. "I want you to stay! We can do this!"

Connie stopped moving. She turned around. "We can't. *You* can't. You're still too angry and I can't go through this anymore."

"Go through what! I'm not angry! I—"

"Do you know what this last week has been like? You say we did all right. All *right!* Do you know what I've been through? Every word I say, every wrong look, you *glare* at me like I put arsenic in your soup! I say the name Glen and you turn to stone. I say the word *boring* and you think I mean you. I feel sorry for Abel and look what you do! Do you know what was on your face when I walked in the door tonight? You *hate* me, Pete! You think you love me! Maybe you do. Maybe you do. Actually, I know you do. But you hate me too. I saw your face tonight and I knew right away. I can't live like this. It hurts too much. It hurts you. It hurts *me.*"

They stood in the freezing wind looking at each other. Pete didn't know what to say. He felt that he still had a speech prepared, that if he just told her about Christmas, about the popcorn and the fireplace, if he gave her Cyrus's little deer, it would fix all this. "I wanted you to stay here for Christmas. With me. So we could work this out."

"There's nothing to work out. Not while you're so angry. I don't want to make you miserable anymore, and I sure as hell don't want to stick around so you can vent your spleen on *me.* I'm leaving for New Jersey the first thing Tuesday morning."

"I see. So you've decided it's all been miserable, it

will always all be miserable, there's no point in giving it another chance."

Connie stepped up to Pete and shook him. "No, it hasn't all been miserable! But I can't live through the parts that are to get to the ones that aren't! Look at right now! You're mad as *hell* at me right now, aren't you? You think you're giving me this big, magnanimous second chance and I'm throwing it back in your face!"

Pete didn't answer her.

Or then again, maybe he did.

Connie laughed shakily. "You think about it," she said. "You let me know if you decide I'm wrong."

Chapter
24

Pete thought about it, all right. All night. Every detail. Every word. It ran through his head like an old movie he'd seen too many times, but all it did was leave him with less of a sense of what had really gone on after all. So she made him miserable when she was around him. So he made *her* miserable when he was around *her*. So what? He was more miserable now than he'd ever been, and not only was she nowhere in sight, there was not even a single prospect of ever seeing her again. She'd go to New Jersey. She'd quit her job. She'd never come back. When he woke in the morning he was all thought out, exhausted, and madder than before. It was Maxine's misfortune to be the first one to cross his path.

Pete walked into his kitchen feeling like the proverbial slimy thing that had just crawled out from under a rock, and there she was, sitting at his kitchen table.

"What are you doing in here?" He buttoned his shirt with angry jerks.

"I just want to know. I mean, I just want to know if you made up your mind. If you're staying here or not."

"I've just about had it with all this crap, Maxine."

Maxine blinked.

"Go to Aunt Ethel's and stop bitching about it, for chrissake."

Maxine jumped up from the table, slamming the chair into the wall as she did so. "Well, who'd want to spend Christmas with an old crab like you, anyway?"

Pete had to admit she had a point.

After Maxine stormed out he sat down in the kitchen chair she had vacated, called Polly, and told her he was going to Florida. Then he called his parents and told them he was going to Maine. It seemed to Pete that nobody seemed to mind a whole lot anymore, that they registered his news and went back to their own distractions of the season before he'd even quite hung up the phone.

Pete walked out into the office and watched Rita look at him once and then look at him again.

"So?" she asked.

"So what?"

Rita gazed thoughtfully at him. She had her scheming face on. "So! Want to come over tomorrow night for a pre-Christmas toast?"

"No thank you."

"Oh, come on, Pete. I'm asking for a reason. I haven't exactly—"

"No—thank—you," Pete repeated from between his teeth.

Rita tightened her lips and changed the subject. "The chief wants to see you."

"Did they find Allison?"

"No. And they won't find her until she wants them to find her. She's a lot smarter than you think."

"I know how smart she is."

"Do you know she has a crush on you?"

"Then she's *not* so smart, is she?" snapped Pete. He

went to the door and yanked it open, banging into Rita's wreath as he went through. A fine shower of dried needles drifted onto the floor. "This thing has started to rot," he said. "How many more days do we have to leave it hanging here, anyway?"

"Three more days."

"Well, it's not going to make it."

"Are *you* going to make it?"

Pete glared at Rita. If there was one thing he really hated, it was Rita when she decided to get cute.

Pete hadn't really planned to see Willy, but a few minutes later he found himself parked in front of the station. Still, he didn't get out of the truck right away. He no longer cared who shot Newby and Evelyn and Jerry and the punch. He no longer even separated any of those shootings in importance. He got out of the truck, walked inside, ignored Ted Ball, and traipsed down the hall to find the chief.

The chief started in all over again about Pete's stupid behavior regarding Allison.

"If that's what you got me here to say, say it fast. I'm in a rush."

"It isn't. But the woman works for you. You saw her last. I want to go over the conversation you had with her again, see if anything strikes a chord, see if we can start at the other end and figure out who she might want to shoot next."

Pete thought about what Rita had said about Allison, but it only made him feel sorrier for Allison than he had before. "She's not going to *shoot* anybody."

"You don't know that. She ran, don't forget. If all she did was shoot out the window at Lupo's, why did she run? You told her we knew she did it. You certainly didn't make it sound like we were going to hang her up by the thumbs."

"I don't care if she ran. She didn't shoot anybody—she's just running to distract us from her father. I told her the first ruse didn't work, and she's trying another, that's all. I think I know her well enough to know that."

"It would be nice if you knew her enough to tell me where she is."

"No," said Pete again. "I don't know her enough for that." He thought again about what Rita had said and dismissed it. He thought about what Connie had said and tried to dismiss that too.

"So if she ran to distract us from her father, she must think her father is guilty of the crimes. And he seems to have the strongest motive."

"No," said Pete, partly because he was in a mood to knock down whatever was in his way today, but partly also because that particular motive no longer seemed anywhere near strong enough. Condos didn't matter. Money didn't matter. What did? Nothing. Not anymore.

Pete was tired. He closed his eyes.

"Hey," said Willy. "Is something the matter with you?"

Pete's eyes snapped open. "I'm tired. And I don't believe condos are behind this crime."

"Oh, you don't. Well, I'll bet you I'm a hell of a lot tireder than you are, and I've got to believe in something. Pease, then."

"No. Cyrus doesn't think much of money. Maybe to lose his land for it seemed like a bad swap, but it was his own decision. And he still has the farm. He likes that farm all right." Suddenly Pete remembered the message on Cyrus's answering machine. He also remembered Glen Newcomb. And Connie.

Pete noticed the chief was squinting at him, and he tried to pull himself back together. "Did you ever decipher that message on the answering machine?"

"No. I've talked to Pease, I've even talked to Newcomb till I'm blue in the face. They still can't place it.'' Willy squinted at him even harder. ''Seems like this Newcomb's suddenly out at the farm an awful lot. And since we're on the subject, are you seeing Connie again or what? Don't I keep running into the two of you at the scene of the crime?''

Pete stood up. ''Now you've hit it. The killer at last. And the next person I'm going to shoot is anyone who mentions her name.''

He couldn't help it. So Connie was right. So he was still mad, plenty mad. But it had gone past wanting to lash out at her or at anyone who mentioned her; now he felt that he could easily murder anyone who crossed his path. It was as if a cold rush of ice water had suddenly flooded his veins.

He drove to Sarah's and was not cheered up to find her bustling around packing for her trip once again. He agreed with Sarah's previous premise now. Why did people go to all this trouble for Christmas? It meant nothing. *Nothing.*

He drove to Beston's Store. He walked up the steps and saw the two huge wreaths on the doors. Was there no escape from it? Was there no place he could hide from all this *joy?* Saudi Arabia. He could go to Saudi Arabia for Christmas! He might as well. It was official now, wasn't it? Even Sarah was leaving. He was going to spend Christmas alone.

So *good.*

Evan Spender nodded to Pete from his spot by the stove. ''Be seeing you at Rita's tomorrow night?''

''Don't count on it.''

''Hey!'' said Ed. ''She's having a party? That's what this place needs! Where's the Christmas cheer this year? Good for Rita, that's what I say!''

Pete walked away from the men at the stove.

Evan followed him. ''Rita's asking Connie. Started

feeling kind of bad she wasn't being more help. What do you think, you—"

Pete whirled around on him. "I tell you what I think. I think Christmas was invented by the travel industry and the Board of Trade and the farmers in Vermont who get rich growing disposable trees instead of food for people to eat."

"Now *there's* a hell of a point!" said Bert. "If you took all those trees and tickets and presents and—"

Pete slammed out of the store.

So he was thinking like Bert Barker now.

If that wasn't depressing, he didn't know what was.

Chapter
25

Connie was drunk and she planned on getting even drunker.

The only trouble was, people kept calling her all the time. The wrong people.

First it was Rita, which was surprising enough in itself. She kept saying things about Pete and Connie that Connie found highly irritating, mostly because she didn't know what the hell Rita was talking about, but Rita kept *insisting* about Connie and Pete and some Christmas toast. Connie had a couple of toasts while she listened to Rita, and then finally she said, "Rita, what the *hell* do you want?"

"What I *want* is for you to come to my house tomorrow at eight," said Rita.

Connie peered into her beer, trying to read its bubbles. Would Pete be there? Would he have thought about what she said? Would he be able to tell her she was wrong, that he wasn't angry anymore, that he wasn't going to make her pay for the rest of her life for this one stupid . . .

"Oh, hell, Rita."

"Well, that's what I *want*," said Rita.

Maybe because Connie wanted *someone* to get what she wanted this year, or maybe because she had missed being friends with Rita, or maybe because she was really, secretly, a schmuck about Christmas, or maybe because she was already missing Pete, she said she'd be there.

The next person who called was Glen Newcomb. Unfortunately, he detected right away that she was drunk. "Thank God," he said. "Now we might get somewhere."

"I have not yet completely pissed my ego away. What do you want? And make it snappy."

"I just want a simple yes or no. I've seen the two of you together everywhere. I just want to know, are you *together* together or just together?"

Connie shivered unexpectedly. "You've seen us where?"

"Everywhere. Come on. I think I have the right to know that much."

Connie tried to think whether or not he had a right to know anything and couldn't think at all. She put down her can of Ballantine Ale, all of a sudden no longer interested in getting drunker. "You've seen us where?"

Glen gave a poor imitation of a ghoul's laugh. "Haven't you heard my footsteps behind you in the street?"

"This isn't funny, Glen."

"Come on. What's going on with you two? Or do I have to ask Pete? I warn you, I'm going to settle this once and for all, one way or the other."

"What the hell isn't settled?"

Glen laughed. "Oh, Pete, for one. The man with nine lives. I just want to know if I have to wait for him to use up all nine before I get another turn."

Connie slammed down the phone. She started to shiver. Then she threw up. She wasn't very good at throwing up, either. It sounded like someone was strangling a moose.

Rita Peck woke up Monday morning, realized it was Monday morning, and groaned. This island. What had started as a simple and, she thought, noble attempt on her part to effect a reconciliation between Pete and Connie was in typical Nashtoba fashion mushrooming into an unwieldy cloud. It had seemed so simple. Christmas was the time of goodwill. She would put aside her resentments of Connie on Pete's behalf and acknowledge his desires. She was confident that if she now put all her energies into helping them instead of hindering them, she would succeed. How could Pete and Connie continue to be upset with each other while they were gathered in front of her fire, candles glowing warmly, with Rita toasting them and their new beginnings in front of the Christmas tree?

It was all Pete's fault, she decided. If he'd just said right out and up front that he was going to be there she wouldn't have had to start bolstering up her defenses. She couldn't have Connie show and Pete not show, now could she? So she began to add in a few people. Evan, of course. And she decided, in a gesture of peace and goodwill, to ask Maxine very nicely if she would please stick around for the party and to bring Todd as well. She invited Andy. She left word with Nate Cox for Allison to join them if she reappeared. She included Sarah Abrew, of course. And then Evan wanted to bring Ed Healey, and somehow or other Bert Barker horned in, and Rita couldn't stand the thought of Bert Barker without at least ten or fifteen other people present to drown him out, and then the phone started ringing, and so the list grew. There were only two more days till Christmas. The island, which had been half shocked out of its Christmas cheer by all the shootings, now looked to Rita's party as a last-ditch chance to get the season back on track. She could feel the communal spirits begin to soar as she collected yet another eager guest. Rita figured that just about everyone on the island would be there.

Except for Pete, of course.

Pete peered between the slowly sweeping windshield wipers and said rotten things under his breath as Sarah Abrew chattered on beside him.

Snow. It wasn't possible. Two days before Christmas and Nashtoba was getting snow? This didn't happen here. Why, of all the years, did it have to happen *this* year, when he would just as soon have gone straight from Thanksgiving to the Fourth of July?

"Of course there won't be any snow in Baltimore, but still, it's nice to have it for my send-off. It used to snow more here. We used to have plenty of White Christmases when I was a girl. It used to snow plenty more— more often and more of it—when it did."

"It'll never last till Christmas."

Sarah didn't so much as glance sideways at him. Her mind was far from Pete now, racing forward to Baltimore or back to her youth, places where his cantankerousness was of no concern.

"Well, it won't." He pulled into the train station and maneuvered the truck in as close to the overhang as he could get it. He got out and ran around to let Sarah out, but she had already snapped open the door and was sliding one tiny foot over the edge. "Here." He caught her elbow and eased her the long way down to the ground. Once she was on firm footing he slid her bag out after her. She took his arm, and they marched amid the scattered flakes in the direction of her train.

Sarah squinted up at the sky. "I suppose you're right. Doesn't look like it'll amount to much."

"No," said Pete. "It won't." But after all, what will?

"About this lottery ticket," said Sarah. "It counts every week? All year?"

"Every week. All year."

Sarah nodded, pleased. "I have a feeling about it. I think I'll win something big. Maybe I'll buy some of those newfangled little Christmas lights next year."

"Thanks for the gloves." Pete flexed his fingers, claustrophobic inside the thick sheepskin lining.

"Leather, so you can clutch onto the wheel if you're driving. But warm for working outside."

"Thanks."

Sarah peered around him, once again moving ahead, leaving him behind. "Is that my train? I like to get on early."

Pete got her on. He settled her case for her and bent stiffly to kiss her good-bye.

He stood on the platform until the train was gone and he was alone.

Alone.

He looked up at the sky, which at four o'clock was already starting to darken, but he could see that the clouds were moving off, that the snow would be stopping soon. The flakes were few and far between. The few inches of snow that had already fallen would probably be gone by morning. *Good.* He got back in the truck and left Bradford for home.

Home. He looked at his watch. Rita's party loomed ahead. Rita was up to something, and Pete knew that whatever it was he wanted no part of it, but he also knew that if he didn't show up, Rita would be deeply disappointed. Pete gave the wheel a nasty jerk on the turn. But so what? Wasn't that the nature of life? Didn't everyone get disappointed in the end?

By the time Pete got to the causeway the snow had stopped altogether, and his tires made gray shadows through the little that had already fallen on the road.

The water had taken on that solid, leaden look that meant the light had left the sky. Pete swung off the causeway onto Shore Road and headed home.

The first thing Pete did was to take down the shedding wreath on the door and throw it in the back of the truck, bound for the next dump run. He felt better at once, and then almost immediately he felt worse.

At eight fifteen Pete found himself dressing begrudgingly for Rita's party. Why? Because he felt so guilty about throwing out her wreath? Pete unhooked his good wool shirt from the hanger and frowned. How far had they come since he'd last worn that shirt at Sarah's tree-trimming party? One step forward. Two back. He should have stayed under Sarah's tree, hiding from Connie. A lot of good it had done him to come out. Even the sniper was still on the loose. Pete frowned even more. How far had they come with *that?* Not very. One person dead, two injured, and Allison on the lam, thanks to him.

As Pete drove toward Rita's his thoughts marched first backward, then forward, in angry stops and starts. The hell with Rita. Why didn't he head straight for the causeway and the world beyond and run away from his own life as others kept running away from him?

The sky had cleared up completely and a nearly full moon lit up the snow below. "The luster of midday"? Bah!

As Pete topped the rise he could see Rita's house below, a single Christmas candle in every small window, the picture window glowing warmly, framing the bodies milling about inside. He couldn't pick out Connie's Triumph from among the herd of cars up and down the street and on the lawn, but now he didn't care whether or not Connie was there. Even if she were there, how could she make him more miserable than she already

Sally Gunning

had? If she wasn't there, the prospect of interacting with Rita and Evan and Maxine and God knows who else was abhorrent enough alone.

Pete wondered if he was the only one on earth right now who wasn't in the Christmas mood. Rita's house seemed to be full of smiling, toasting, singing, kissing *schmucks*. He thought of Sarah's and the scene through her window that night. What Pete needed was to find a roomful of the other ones, the ones who were sick to death of this stupid holiday—the Grinches, the Scrooges, the others with the ice water in their veins.

The hell with it. Pete swung the truck around and headed for Shore Road.

Jack Whiteaker had finished the decorating of his hotel. Each white column was wrapped in holly and red velvet, and he had spotlighted each one. Pete's thoughts being what they were, he felt an instant outrage at the sight of all that Christmas cheer right across from the dead Newby's bait shop. He sped the truck past. If he were Ozzie he'd go over there, rip down the holly and ribbons, and blast those big lights into hell! If he were Ozzie he'd . . .

Pete slowed the truck. If he were Ozzie, *is* that what he would do? If he were Ozzie. If he were Ozzie. Or even if he weren't! Pete's mind raced on. If he were anyone who had had it with Christmas, who couldn't stand the sight of someone else having fun while he was alone or in pain . . .

Images flashed past Pete's brain at warp speed, images of every sniper scene that had already come and gone.

Sarah's tree-trimming party.

The carol sing at Beston's.

Jerry's Christmas lights on the little tree.

The bowl of Christmas punch! *Maybe he was after the punch*, Connie had said.

Could it be?

Yes. *Yes!* Wasn't Pete himself feeling it—didn't he almost want to kill Christmas himself this year? Couldn't some other less balanced soul have taken it all the way to that horrible end, have tried to shoot out Christmas wherever he found it—at Sarah's, at Beston's, at Jerry's, at the school? And even Mrs. Potts's crazy wreath for her birds—didn't that fit, too?

Pete whipped the truck through a U-turn in Martelli's parking lot and raced down Shore Road toward the police station. This was it. It *had* to be it! Someone crazed by Christmas. Oh, he'd known all along that all these so-called connections were too farfetched—that they were stretching points as far as they could stretch them just because there were no other reasonable motives in sight, because science had taken them only so far, but not nearly far enough. This new theory, this Christmas-crazed-sniper theory, fit without any effort at all. All the chief had to do was figure out the scene of the next big Christmas festivity and—

Suddenly Pete was shot through with both the coldness of fear and the heat of fury.

Rita's.

Rita's would be the target tonight—he was sure of it. Rita's party was the first real holiday event since that disastrous party at the school. Rita's. Most of the people he loved were going to be at Rita's tonight. Which one was going to be the victim?

Suddenly Pete remembered the rise. He had paused on that very hill not moments ago and had looked down at Rita's glowing window! There it was—the perfect sniper hill, looking down over the perfect target!

Pete almost drove straight past the police station in the direction of Rita's, but he considered what his charging after Allison on his own had done. He forced himself to slow, to turn, to do what was responsible and safe and correct and in the long run much more likely to succeed. He pulled right up to the station, bolted out of the truck, and without so much as looking at Ted Ball, he tore down the hall and into the chief's office.

The chief was there. Pete took the time to breathe in once. He told the chief about the sniper and Christmas and Paul Roose tracking the sniper's haunts to the high ground. He told him about the little hill that overlooked Rita's house. The chief seemed to know just what Pete meant, just *where* Pete meant. He wasted no time. Pete found himself scrambling after the chief, following the Scout in his truck back toward the causeway and Rita's house. Claustrophobic fingers or not, Pete began to wish he had Sarah's gloves with him. His hands slid around the wheel in their own sweat.

Chapter
26

At eight thirty Connie found herself dressed and ready and walking out the door for Rita's party. Connie always prided herself on being able to meet a person halfway. True, Rita had been a real pill to her ever since she had left Pete, and Connie had been pretty hurt that Rita hadn't even tried to see the other side. But if Rita was going to invite her to a party, Connie was going to go. She refused to think about Pete and whether or not he'd be there. If he was, he was. If he wasn't, he was missing a chance to see just how adult and forgiving and half-wayish a person could be.

Connie walked out into the night and squinted at the starkness of the white and black around her. The moon-light arrowed down to meet the snow. Black claws of tree branches stood out against the glare like a grave-yard scene from Dickens. The air was dead and cold. Connie shivered. She squeezed into the Triumph and fumbled with her keys, annoyed to see that her hands were shaking. What was spooking her this way? She took three deep breaths and started over. It was her first trip out that day and the little car took its time coming to, but finally she was under way.

But why did she feel like looking over her shoulder all the time?

Connie never used to be a fearful person. She couldn't see the sense in fearing those unknown things that might never happen, things that, even if they did happen, might not be all that scary after all. And she couldn't see the sense in fearing the known thing, either. The known was there, no matter how you felt about it. Why waste precious steam being afraid of it? It was much better to commit that energy to outsmarting it.

So what was this, this weird unease? It had all started with this stupid sniper and her fears about Pete. Yes, that was something she had been fearful of—someone harming Pete—but Pete was nowhere around now. So what was it that was setting her off tonight? Was it because of one ridiculous phone call from Glen New-comb? Of course he wasn't watching her or following her. Glen's phone call had been the result of a sense of humor in need of a tune-up. Connie tossed her head to give her brain a good shake. No. Clearly, she was the one whose sense of humor needed tuning up! Hell, even if he *were* following her, what was he going to do—shoot her?

Connie's cheeks and hands began to tingle. *Shoot her.* Shoot her?

Suddenly Connie's old fears about Pete and the new unnamed fears of the night began to find common ground.

What if Glen were following *Pete?*

Connie slowed the car. Sarah's. Beston's. Beggs's roof. The school. Lupo's. Pete had been present or could have been expected to be present at every one. Hadn't she said that very thing to Pete before? The one thing she hadn't done was find a motive for anyone to harm Pete. Connie shook her head again. She still hadn't found one. True, Glen had called her—twice now—just to find out if she and Pete were or were not back together again. Why? Because he wanted her to come back to him. He'd said as much, hadn't he? He had said he'd settle this one way or the other. What did he *mean?* He had called Pete the man with nine lives. Connie had assumed he meant Pete's nine chances with *her,* but what if he'd been referring instead to his having escaped death five times with four shots left to go? Four *shots.* But did all cats get the full nine? That was the question. Weren't there some cats with bad luck, bad genes, short life lines?

All of a sudden Connie snorted out loud. She was losing her mind. Cats. Life lines. Shots. *Glen Newcomb,* trying to kill Pete. Because of *her?* No way. Connie took two deep breaths and sped toward Rita's road.

She barely noticed the first car she passed. The second one was Pete's truck. The third one was Glen Newcomb's Toyota.

Chapter
27

Pete peered into the woods, one minute grateful for the visibility provided by the moon and the next minute cursing it as he imagined human shapes in every shadow. They were at the rise, but the question was, was the sniper? And if so, just where on the rise? The thick scrub and twisted trees were plenty thick enough for cover from the road. There would have to be a place where he would come out of that to get a clear shot at Rita's. Would they find that place in time? By now Rita's party was probably in full swing. Historically speaking, that was when the sniper seemed to strike.

The chief pulled off the road up ahead, and Pete pulled in after him. The chief was following an old, half-grown track of some kind that Pete hadn't noticed before. The truck bumped its way after the Scout into the brush as far as it could go. The Scout kept going. Pete got out and scrambled after the chief on foot.

When Pete finally came abreast of the Scout, the chief was just returning on foot from further up the track. "Okay. You go back now. Go home. I've got him. I'm calling in for backup now."

"What?" But even in his amazement, Pete was flooded with relief. Willy had got him. But where? How? Pete peered around the chief into the thicket and caught the gleam of a car's roof through the trees. The chief leaned into the Scout and reached for the radio. A twig snapped somewhere off to Pete's right, but before he could swing around, something blacker than the trees behind it loomed up from the direction in which the chief had just come. It came closer. The moonlight struck its face. Paul Roose.

"Hey, Will," whispered Pete. "It's okay, Paul's here already."

But to Pete's amazement the chief whirled on his deputy, and before Pete could say a word, the chief's gun was out and Paul was spread-eagled against the car.

"What in the—"

"Get out of here!" barked Willy. "Now!"

Pete didn't move. He stood there and stared as the chief started to read Paul his rights.

"What in the holy hell, Will—"

"I said go! Get that truck out of there."

Paul Roose looked sideways at Pete. His face was half in shadow, but the half that Pete could see was cracked with Paul's same old cryptic grin.

Pete went.

Chapter
28

Connié continued on for some distance before it really sank in that she had just passed Pete's old blue truck followed by Glen Newcomb's silver Toyota. Once that fact had sunk in she tried to come up with some logical explanation for it, but failed miserably. Glen Newcomb didn't even live here anymore. True, now that Cyrus was back, he'd been around a lot more, but still, he wouldn't be driving around the island in the dead of night for his health, now, would he?

Glen's words over the phone wires began to ring over and over in Connie's ears, and with each turn of her tires things that had seemed so ludicrous minutes before now began to take on a more plausible cast. Glen had sounded pretty bitter over the phone. And after all, blame had been placed wrongly before. Suppose he decided to blame Pete for the failure of his and Connie's affair? Of course it was completely unfair, but who ever said life was fair? Suppose, just for argument's sake, that Glen thought Pete was the only thing that stood in his way with Connie. Of course it made no sense for Glen to think that by disposing of Pete Connie would return to him, but who ever said life made sense? Glen had talked about doing something drastic this time. He had told Connie she was going to need her tears later. She had assumed he'd been referring to the lousy odds of Pete and her ever making it. Had he really been predicting that *Pete* wouldn't make it?

Connie turned the Triumph around in the middle of the bushes that hugged the road at that spot, barely aware of the fingernails-on-blackboard effect of bayberry branches on paint. She raced back down the narrow road. The first thing she saw was the moonlight glinting off the silver roof of Glen's car where he had pulled off onto the shoulder, but Pete's truck was nowhere in sight. Connie bumped the Triumph up over the side of the road and braked to a stop behind Glen's car. She peered into the shadows, but could see no one. She got out. The sound of her car door must have brought Glen back from wherever he'd been, because suddenly there he was, a long, thin shadow separating itself from the dark of the woods.

"Connie! What are you doing here?"

"What are *you* doing here? God, if I ever thought for a minute—"

Glen's teeth flashed in the moonlight. "Yes, if you ever *thought* for a minute, things would have turned out quite differently, wouldn't they?"

Connie had just about had it with Glen. She charged at him, grabbed him by the front of his jacket, and shook him. "I swear to God, if you've hurt him I'll kill you! Where is he? You followed him here, didn't you?"

Glen's long fingers plucked at Connie's fists but she dug into the folds of his coat like a tick, refusing to be plucked off.

"I only followed him because I was on my way to see him and passed him on Shore Road. If you would

223

kindly stop rattling me around and explain yourself, I believe we could—''

"Explain *my*self! Me! You're trying to shoot him and you want me to explain myself!"

Connie could see Glen's features clearly in the moonlight only inches from her own. All of a sudden the ludicrous half smile dropped from his face. His hands fell to his sides.

"*Shoot* him. Shoot him. I followed him to ask him a simple question. The same simple question I attempted to ask you. But I think I'm beginning to see that the answer is of no consequence now. It never was, was it?" Glen lifted his hands, this time using them more successfully to unleash Connie from his coat, and then held both their hands briefly in front of his face, staring at them as if they were the hands of strangers. "And here I thought we knew each other."

Connie yanked herself out of his grasp. "*Knew* each other! We hardly even *recognize* each other on the street! For chrissake, Glen, where is he? Is he—"

From among the blackened brambles someplace near at hand they heard a shout, a shout that Connie *did* know. It was all she needed. She charged into the brush in what she thought was the direction of the sound, only half aware that Glen chose to take a different route.

Chapter
29

Pete turned to leave the woods on the police chief's instructions, but not because he agreed with him. Paul Roose the sniper? No. Not possible. Pete had known Paul most of his life. He knew that Paul had changed over the past year, starting with the new chief's arrival—knew that Paul had not exactly been helpful to the new chief—but to become a murderer just to confound the man further was too much, even for Paul.

But what could Pete do about it? Better to leave them—better to let them return to the station, where things would be sorted out in the clear light of day. Pete turned his back on the policemen, partly, he knew, because he couldn't stand to look at them any longer. The scene he had just witnessed could only mean destruction for one of these men. Obviously, if the chief were right, this was the end of Paul, but if he were wrong, wouldn't this be the end of Willy? It would be the end of his career on the island, anyway, once this story got out, and Pete had no doubt that Paul would waste no time getting the story out. But there was nothing Pete could do. He trod over the snow-covered ruts toward his truck. The best thing for him to do was to return to the station and wait there for the two men. Maybe back in the familiar confines of the station, out of this uncanny moonlight and unreal shadows, he could talk some sense into them. Or into *one* of them, at any rate.

Pete lashed out at a tree branch that snagged his collar and started as it gave a loud snap—a snap that suddenly jogged him back to his original premise.

How had he let the macabre scene behind him divert him from his course? If Paul was not the sniper, as Pete believed he was not, his original theory remained the same. Rita's party. The rise. The sniper lurking in the woods. The police chief now had his hands full behind him. It was up to Pete to follow through. It was up to him to do something and to do it fast.

Pete tried to think it through further. What would be the best course from here? He could return to the road and start again. It shouldn't be hard in the snow to find the tracks of a man or a vehicle entering the woods. Had that been what Willy had done—seen tracks and followed them—the tracks of Paul Roose? Pete had been behind Willy, following the chief's tracks. He couldn't speak for whatever tracks had been there before. Was that why *Paul* was here? Had *Paul* pulled into the woods following tracks of his own? Pete turned around in confusion, but the way back was blocked by Paul's car and Willy's Scout. Besides, any sniper in this immediate vicinity would be long gone by now. It was getting crowded around here. Better to return to the road and look again. Pete set off along the old track, but then stopped and thought again. He was wasting time covering the same track twice. Why not return to the road by some parallel course, thereby covering that much more new ground? Pete turned off into the woods at a forty-five-degree angle and pushed on, careful to make as little sound as possible, straining his ears and his eyes ahead, behind, left, right.

Soon Pete could feel the ground falling away beneath him. This was no good. He was coming off the rise. But wait. The sniper needed high ground, sure, but he also needed a clear shot. From here, deep in the trees, he wasn't going to get *any* kind of a shot, let alone a clear one. If he moved toward the face of the hill, didn't it thin out? Wouldn't he be high enough and the view clear enough for a prime shot at Rita's if he kept heading this way? Yes. Pete could tell already that the woods were getting thinner, better to see through, but at the same time, all that much better to nestle into with a car or a truck. Wasn't he moving closer to the road all the time, but further from the part of the road where he and the chief and Paul had entered? Yes, he was. Suddenly he saw another gleam, another shaft of moonlight on some sort of a vehicle's roof. His feet less sure and steady beneath him in the snow, he pushed over a last, abrupt drop in the rise and found everything just as he had scripted it.

The woods ended abruptly in a clearing just over the lip of the rise. The road in front of Rita's wound black below it, the white landscape spread evenly from the road to the yellow glow of Rita's windows.

The back of the man in front of Pete was nothing but a shadow against the white snow, a shadow with one elongated black arm made by a rifle that was aimed down the hill toward Rita's house.

"No!" shouted Pete. He sprinted forward into the clearing. The shadow whipped around. The moonlight danced along the rifle as it dipped toward the ground and lit the face above it.

"Abel!"

Abel Cobb looked at Pete, saw that it was Pete, and slowly raised the rifle again until it was level with Pete's face. Behind them something crashed through the brush. Abel looked toward the sound, swinging the gun as well as his eyes. Pete charged into him.

"Pete!" It was Connie, shouting from behind him. *Connie*, with a man's voice shouting in answer from someplace further back.

Pete grabbed for Abel's gun. He could feel the weight of Abel on its other end, but it was a weight of little consequence. Pete's own adrenaline tore the gun from Abel's grip with ease, swinging it away from them as it went off. That's all he did, swing the gun away from them. He couldn't understand why the next thing he heard was Connie screaming—or why her body suddenly thudded into the snow at his feet.

Chapter
30

It was ten o'clock in the morning, the morning of Christmas Eve. One more long day to go, and then the very longest day yet. Pete sat in the police station across from the police chief, carving up the chief's desk with the blade of his Swiss army knife.

It was all over. Connie was gone. Abel Cobb was locked up. Paul Roose had quit.

"It's not your fault," said Willy.

"It's not *your* fault," said Pete.

"Goddammit, it isn't!" Willy suddenly shouted, jumping up from his chair. "He didn't tell me a damned thing! He went out on his own. He ran his own investigation without coordinating it within the department. He tried to show me up. From day one he knew too much. It's not my fault that I came to the conclusion that the only way he could know so much was because he was the sniper himself!"

Pete gouged an especially impressive hunk of wood out of Willy's desk and looked up at him. "It's *not* your fault."

Willy sank down in his chair again, and for a minute nobody spoke. "Where is she?" he asked at last.

"New Jersey."

"Home for the holidays," said Willy, and then he laughed a bitter laugh.

Now Pete jumped up. "I thought she was *dead*," he said. "I heard the gun go off—I *felt* the gun go off—and there she was, down on the ground. I stood there looking at her, thinking it was all over, and then she rolled over and started *yelling* at me. She thinks I did it on purpose."

"She doesn't think you did it on purpose."

"She thinks I'm that furious with her. She thinks I *subconsciously* turned around at the sound of her voice and aimed the gun right at her. That's why she hit the ground, because she actually thought I was going to *shoot* her."

"She didn't really think you were going to shoot her."

Pete stopped pacing around behind his chair and slumped back into it instead. "Well, she sure as hell made it sound like she did."

"It's not your fault," said Willy.

'It's not *your* fault," said Pete. "You had plenty of reasons. And Paul Roose hasn't once played you fair. He knows it, too—that's why he's not laying any blame, that's why he's keeping quiet about what went on in the woods."

"You're right about that. Ever since I came here, he dragged his feet every step of the way. He didn't do squat around here. Then along came this murder. What was the first thing that happened? Everyone was there at Abrew's but Paul Roose. Then there was the night you found the bullet. I wrapped that bullet tight. I locked that bullet in the safe. All of a sudden Paul Roose showed up at Abrew's with information about its caliber, its jacketing, information no one but me knew at that time. How was I to know Jean Martell unlocked the safe, unwrapped the bullet, and showed it to him? She thinks *she* runs things around here."

"And he knew a lot about guns. All that stuff about trajectory—"

"He knew a *hell* of a lot about guns, about military weapons, about ammunition—more than he ever learned from being a cop. *And* he was a World War Two vet. And he was never present at the actual time of the shootings, but would show up pretty damned soon after it was over. Look at the school. He was right out there, right on the rise. How was I to know he was starting to figure out the sniper's pattern by then? He didn't tell *me*. He wanted to do it on his own. He wanted to show me up. And don't forget, his prints were all over Pease's M-1, as well as the shotgun shell. And how about that bullet Jack Whiteaker found? One of ours. Paul pocketed it, never said a word to me, then you tell me about it and I lay into Paul and what does he come up with? He thought Ted must have been potshotting at tin cans and didn't want to get him into trouble. And Paul found that shotgun shell in five seconds at Lupo's. In the *fog*. How the hell did he do that?"

"Lucky, I guess."

Willy snorted. "And then last night. You charged in here with this story about Rita's, dragged me off to the woods, and there he was, lurking in the dark."

Pete shook his head.

"There were too many coincidences," Willy went on, obsessed with it now. "Newby Dillingham and Evelyn Waxman both opposed to the condos. The Pease land deals. All these vets with their souvenir weapons. Even Beggs threatening Cox. What are the odds of all that going on in a town this size?"

Pete had known all along that on Nashtoba the odds

for these bizarre connections were much higher than the odds against, but he wisely remained silent.

It didn't seem to bother the chief any. "And *Abel Cobb*," he continued. "He's got nothing to do with condos *or* World War Two. Nothing."

"Still," said Pete, "I should have figured it was Abel. I should have figured it was Abel a long time ago. The message on the machine. I'd heard Abel's voice twenty times at the bar—drunk, sure, but I knew I knew it. I just couldn't place it. And that part about not moving until he sells. It made no sense that someone would not move in order to sell a *gun*. Paul knew it must have meant something like selling a house. Abel's house was for sale. He was cleaning it out attic to cellar. Abel's dad was a colonel in World War Two. I *knew* that. *Paul* knew that. *Everyone* knew that. Abel found that old M-1 in his father's attic, complete with the old ball ammunition. He called up Cyrus, figuring to sell it, but Cyrus never called him back. Cyrus didn't need two M-1 Garands. Finally Abel decided to use it himself. Paul knew Abel was some sort of hot shot in Vietnam. *I* knew Abel was. I *knew* he could shoot. He wasn't on the gun club lists around here because he only just got here. Paul Roose followed Abel up to that hill. He parked in deep on the other side of the rise and was going to move in on Abel the minute he got set up."

"Until I came along."

"Well, at least you were there to corral Abel."

"At least you caught on to the motive. Abel Cobb got kicked out by his wife, quit his job, came back to Nashtoba to sell out. He found his father's gun. At first he tried to sell, but then Christmas started closing in, and it started to get to him, just like you said. All this Christmas cheer, and him all alone."

Pete jabbed viciously at the desk.

"And you were right about Nate Cox," said the chief.

"He *can't* shoot. I finally found a witness who remembered him at the rifle range because he was so bad. Nate Cox says he heard about the shot that killed Newby and was impressed. He had nothing else to do the next day. He hit the rifle range with his father's old gun to see what he could do without Frank Lake marking up bull's-eyes from the pit."

Willy fell silent.

Pete jabbed into the desk.

"But hell," said Willy finally. "At least I found Allison."

Pete looked up. "Where?"

"Boyfriend's."

"Boyfriend's?"

"Well, he's her boyfriend now. She called the brother of a friend who lives in Boston. He picked her up at the Bradford airport, leaving her car there to lead us off the track. He took her up north. Somewhere between here and New Hampshire they fell in love."

Et tu, Allison, thought Pete. She'd probably never come back. She wouldn't be getting her sweater if she didn't, but then again, she wouldn't be *needing* her sweater, now that she had love to keep her warm. "So if I'd called you in when I should have, Allison would never have gotten off Cape Hook."

The chief shrugged.

"Did she say anything? About Lupo's, I mean?"

The chief nodded. "You were right all along. She admitted to shooting out the window at Lupo's with Martell's shotgun. She insisted she was very careful that no one would get hurt. When you wised up to it she panicked and ran, hoping to convince us she'd done all the shooting, to distract us from her father that way. She said her father was close to breaking, not only financially, but emotionally as well."

Pete dug away at the desk in silence, immersed in his

own gloom, but suddenly Willy seemed to notice what he was doing.

"Hey!" He jumped up and grabbed the knife, but took one look at Pete's face and seemed to think better of whatever else he was thinking of saying.

"Come on," he said instead. "Let's get out of here. It's Christmas Eve. What do you say, Christmas in Connecticut?"

Pete stood up. "No. Thanks, though."

Pete walked out of the station alone. Outside he saw that he was right about one other thing—the morning's fog was just lifting, taking with it the last remnants of yesterday's snow.

Chapter
31

Christmas Day was now only hours away. Pete cruised slowly down Shore Road on his way to Rita's house, the two small boxes wrapped in silver paper nestled among the empty coffee cups, crumpled Dorito bags, and ravaged sports page on the seat of the truck. The holiday garb of the Whiteaker Hotel stood out even more garishly against the leaden water of the harbor and the even bleaker gray of the sky.

A lone figure in a navy watch cap and gun-metal gray jacket was just stepping off the dock in front of the hotel, crossing the parking lot to his shop.

Ozzie Dillingham.

Pete swung his truck in behind Ozzie and got out.

Ozzie stopped walking. They turned to face the harbor together. Neither man spoke as they gazed out to sea.

"Abel Cobb," said Ozzie finally, bitterly. "And he wasn't even after my brother at all."

Pete shook his head. "Or Evelyn, or Jerry."

"Or that lousy punch," said Ozzie, the intensity of his expression little varied between the subject of punch or brother, but Pete figured he was one of the few people who understood. The difference between life and death, punch and brother probably *had* been only one beer more or less at Lupo's.

"Listen," said Pete, but found there was, after all, nothing more to say. "So," he said instead. "You selling out or not?"

Ozzie squinted at the shoreline. "Been thinking about that. Been thinking what I'd do with a half million dollars."

Pete looked down the beach and saw, instead of the slender lip of sand and dune, condominiums, minimalls, and health clubs. Some obscure piece of Pete that hadn't already sunk to rock bottom sunk there right then.

"And you know what I figure I'd like about best? A nice little bait shop on a harbor somewhere."

Pete looked at Ozzie.

Ozzie looked back at Pete, and Pete could have sworn there was finally a little of his dead brother's twinkle in his eye.

"Merry Christmas," Ozzie said.

Rita and Maxine were in their usual day-before-Christmas tizzy. Maxine, her previous animosity miraculously forgotten, was busy piling up suitcases near the door and singing "Rudolph the Red-Nosed Reindeer" off-key. Rita raced by in one direction with pieces of Scotch tape stuck to her fingers and stopped only long enough to look at Pete with moisture-filled eyes as she said, "Abel *Cobb?*"

Pete nodded. Rita dashed meticulous scarlet fingernails across her tears and left the room. When she returned she was trailing red Christmas ribbon from one shoe.

"Well, I am sorry about last night. But at least you're here now. Maxine, take that bag of presents and put them in the car. No, not that one—that one's for Pete. Did you turn off the kettle? Is the back door locked? Did you pack your vitamins?"

"I turned. I locked. I packed." As Maxine flew by she smacked Pete in the back with a long, thin package that felt like it contained a double-edged sword. "Come *on*, Mom, let's go! Here, Pete! This is from us. You're going to love this. Where's mine?"

Pete handed over the smaller of his two silver boxes and attempted to respond appropriately as she tried on the earrings in front of the mirror, shook her head, and laughed with delight at the dancing stars.

Pete opened the rectangular box that Maxine had thrust into his hands and pulled out a thick gray sweatshirt. A pen-and-ink-type sketch of his little cottage was silk-screened across the front, with FACTOTUM written below.

"Thanks."

Pete looked at it some more. It looked just like his cottage. It *felt* just like his cottage. *"Thanks,"* he said again. He thrust the second silver box at Rita, who opened it up, unfolded Ozzie's makeshift gift certificate for the day's sail, and threw her arms around Pete's neck.

That fast, their Christmas together was over. Pete helped carry the boxes and bags to the car, Rita and Maxine ran back twice each for things they had forgotten or thought they had forgotten, then they climbed into the little Dodge Omni, packed to bursting for a stay of two nights and one day. Pete told them to drive carefully, to say hello to Aunt Ethel, to have fun, but they waved abstractly back, their minds already on the trip ahead. Pete climbed into his truck, the sweatshirt in its box placed carefully on the seat beside him, and followed the Dodge as far as the causeway. He watched the car brave the wooden planks and diminish on the far side.

"Aunt Ethel, here they come," Pete warned out loud, and headed for home, alone.

It was late afternoon by now, and the little house was dark and still. Even the marsh seemed empty of all life, the birds apparently having all settled down for the night. He pushed open his door, bare of all decoration, flicked on the light, and looked at Rita's desk. No holly. He looked at the box with the sweatshirt in it that he still held in his hands.

Pete put the box down suddenly, turned around, and went back outside. He reached into the back of the truck and pulled out a large pair of pruning shears. He crossed his lawn to the edge of the scrub pines, selected a small branch, and snipped it off. He returned inside, plucked the box off Rita's desk, went straight to his kitchen, and rummaged around under the sink until he found an empty jar. He filled it with water, plunged the tree branch in, and centered the tree in the middle of the kitchen table. He took the bow off the sweatshirt box, attached it to the top of the tree, removed the sweatshirt, and pulled the warm fleece over his head. He grabbed a kettle off the hook on the wall, poured oil into the bottom, and added a handful of dried corn. Once the corn was popped he poured it into his favorite red and white bowl and grabbed a beer from the refrigerator. He sat down in front of his little tree, tipped back his chair, and put his feet up on the sill.

The phone began to ring.

Pete snapped his chair back down to the ground. It was Christmas Eve. Who would be calling him now? He considered the various possibilities. By now, he knew, his mother would have called Polly and his cover would be blown. It could be his mother, or it could be Polly, calling to yell at him for engineering a Christmas alone. Or it could be Rita, stuck on the road with a flat tire and a screaming daughter. Or it could be Sarah, reminding him to pick up her mail, check her doors, water her plants. It could even be Willy with one more loose end to tie up, one more blame to be placed.

Or it could be Connie.

And why would Connie call? To apologize for thinking he could ever, subconsciously or not, try to shoot her? To ask him if he'd thought about what she had said, to ask him if he was still angry with her after all?

Pete tensed, waiting for the usual rush of angry ghosts that followed thoughts of Connie, and was surprised to find the only image that came to mind was that of Connie lying motionless in the snow. What had happened? Had that one long instant when he had supposed her to be dead finally cured him of the rest?

The phone rang and rang.

It was true. He *wasn't* angry anymore. What he really was was tired—tired in muscle and bone and brain. Suddenly Pete realized that he wasn't up to picking up the phone, no matter which of all those much-loved, persistent people it might be on the other end. Connie *wasn't* dead. There would be time later to do whatever it was that he had to do. Right now he wasn't up to thinking about it, wasn't up to talking to a single solitary human soul.

Pete looked out his kitchen window at the growing dark, at the peace and solitude of the marsh and the sea beyond. He tipped back his chair, put his feet back on the sill, popped open his beer, and unplugged the phone.

Chapter
32

Ed Healey sat on Beston's porch in the cold and smoothed down his snow-white beard as it swayed with the wind. Ed Healey swayed a little too, but that wasn't the fault of the wind.

"Abel Cobb," he said, and shook his head so that the silver bell at the end of his red stocking cap jingled.

"That's what they *say* happened," said Bert Barker. "But if you want to know what *I* think, I think there's something fishy going on!"

Evan Spender winked at Ed, and Ed's blue eyes gave an answering twinkle. "So, you're going to your daughter's again, Bert?"

"Sure I'm going to my daughter's again. Now what I want to know is this. Who's going to shoot somebody over *Christmas?*"

"Oh, I don't know. Did you give your wife her present yet?" asked Evan.

Ed Healey laughed, and his several bellies under the red wool coat shook.

Bert glared at Evan. "Of course I didn't give my wife her present yet! It isn't even Christmas yet! She'll get her present tomorrow, assuming she doesn't do anything in the meantime to louse it up! Now what I want to know is this—if everything's so all-fired neat as a pin on this Cobb thing, what's Paul Roose quitting the department for just like that?"

Evan looked at his watch and stood up. "I think I'll head home, I've got a jug of Cyrus's cider in the fridge. How about it, Ed? Bert? A Christmas glass of cider?"

"Bah!" said Bert. "I'll bet you ten dollars that's last year's cider! I told you all along, they should just get off their butts and get out there and catch that sniper in the act—none of this sitting around trying to figure it out through science!"

"They caught him in *one* act, sure," said Evan. "But it's that science that'll get him on the murder."

"Of *course* it's last year's cider," said Ed. "What'd be the good of it if it wasn't?"

"And another thing!" Bert kept on. "If the chief's the one who found Cobb the way they say he did—"

"How about you, Ed?" asked Evan. "A little cider?"

Ed Healey heaved himself up off the bench, straightening his silver belt buckle. "What, tonight? Christmas Eve? I've got work to do, Ev!"

Evan chuckled. "So you do. My mistake." He raised his hand to Bert. "Have a good time at your daughter's, Bert."

"Well, I might if she'd once learn to cook a turkey!" Bert hollered after them. "And I'd like to know something else! Why's Ozzie so fired up about that lousy bait shop all of a sudden?"

Ed Healey tottered sideways on his way down the porch steps, but Evan Spender caught him by his wide black belt and steadied him up.

"Ho, ho, ho and a bottle of rum!" Ed sang out down in the street.

Evan whispered something to him.

Ed Healey stopped walking and tipped his beard up to the darkening sky. "I mean, 'Ho, ho, ho, *Me-e-e-e-rry* Christmas'!"

CIRCUMSTANCES UNKNOWN

A NOVEL OF SUSPENSE

JONELLEN HECKLER

He crossed the street slowly and entered Central Park near the boat pond. Children and their parents ringed it, operating remote controls on a fleet of toy sailing ships....<u>Look how they close the circle, these people, making fences of their devotion, shutting him out</u>. In the photograph in his pocket, the family was smiling....Tim. Deena. Jon, age five. Soon, they would pay for the sin of their pride. Soon, they would learn that it all can end in a flash...in flawlessly planned, seemingly accidental death....

POCKET

B O O K S

Available in hardcover from Pocket Books March 1993